U0000795

經典小說
Classic Novels

經典如飛颺的雪花
讓人沈醉在生命的永恆

————————

聖誕頌歌

A CHRISTMAS CAROL IN PROSE,
BEING A GHOST STORY OF CHRISTMAS

狄更斯 ◎著
顏湘如 ◎譯

臺灣商務印書館

人物介紹

艾布內茲・施顧己

經營「施顧己與馬利」商號，在生意場上貪得無厭，沉默、封閉與孤僻，人生唯一樂事是在辦公室處理帳目、攢積存摺上的財富。

弗瑞德

施顧己的外甥，為人開朗和善，相信聖誕節為人生所帶來的好處；認為唯有這一天，男男女女才會不約而同地敞開封閉的心，真心將那些身分卑微的人視為陪伴自己步向人生旅途終點的伴侶。

雅各・馬利

施顧己七年前已逝的合夥人，在七年後的聖誕夜，以「鬼魂」的身分重新出現。

鮑伯・克萊契

施顧己商號的夥計。一個星期賺取十五先令的微薄薪資。以無盡的慈愛照護雙腳殘廢的兒子「小提姆」。

三個聖誕精靈

過去的聖誕精靈──在第一天裡一點的鐘聲響起時出現在施顧己的房間。穿著一件潔白長袍，手裡握著一把鮮綠冬青，頭頂上迸射出一束明亮的光芒。

現在的聖誕精靈──在第二天夜裡一點的鐘聲響起時出現。身上只穿著一件有白色皮毛滾邊的深綠色袍子，一雙赤腳。頭頂上戴了一頂冬青花冠，冠上隨意裝飾幾根閃亮小冰柱，腰間配帶一柄古老劍鞘。

未來的聖誕精靈──在第三天夜裡十二點的鐘聲敲完最後一響時出現。裹著一件深黑色長袍的幽靈，蓋住了頭、臉、身形；高大、威嚴，在它行經的空氣中，散播出幽暗與神祕。

這是一個讓讀者又哭又笑的故事——無論讀者心地善良或者心腸冷酷，作者都給予了關懷、對他們敞開心胸……如同擺放在國王面前的一道佳肴。

——倫敦文學雜誌《雅典娜》（*Athenaeum*）

如果說聖誕節那古老溫馨好客的傳統，以及它所建立社會慈善的風尚正面臨傾頹的危機，那麼能夠作為中流砥柱力挽此一狂瀾者，也就是本書了。

作者的大名使讀者心生慈悲，光是讀了前面幾頁，就足以使人雀躍。

——詩人兼幽默大師湯姆士・胡德（Thomas Hood），一八四四年書評

此書有益於社稷，讀過這本書的男男女女也從中得到了關懷。最後兩個

與我談論此書的讀者都是女性，她們兩人彼此不認識，也都不認識作者，但是她們異口同聲說道：「願上帝保佑他。」

這本書看上去是那麼小那麼薄，但卻是英國的財富。

——威廉・薩克萊（William Thackeray），《弗雷澤雜誌》（*Fraser's Magazine, 1844*）

讀起來感覺很好，精心設計的內容也對社會有正面的影響。

——書評家西奧多・馬汀（Theodore Martin）

來自四面八方的郵件，寫信的人形形色色，而且都是陌生人，信裡描述他們自己的家和家中的壁爐，也寫到這本聖誕頌歌是如何在這些地方被大聲朗誦、是如何被收藏在小架子上，以便與其他書籍有所區別。

——狄更斯（Carles Dickens）

在這本充滿幻象的薄書中，我試著傳遞一種觀念的幻影，而這種觀念絕不能讓我的讀者生自己的氣、生彼此的氣、生季節的氣或生我的氣。但願這樣的幻影能帶著愉快的氣氛縈繞在讀者的屋裡，誰也不想驅散它。

他們忠實的僕人及朋友

查爾斯・狄更斯

一八四三年，十二月

馬利的靈魂

1

首先要說的是：馬利死了。這是毫無疑問的。牧師、教堂書記、葬儀社的人與喪主，都已經在他的死亡登記簿上簽名。施顧己也簽了名：在交易所，只要有了施顧己的簽名，就等於是有了信用保證。老馬利已經像門釘一樣死僵了。

別會錯意了！我這麼說並不代表我個人有什麼證據，可以證明門釘比其他事物更死氣沉沉。依我之見，我倒覺得棺木釘才是金屬之中死得最透徹的一樣。不過這個比喻蘊藏著老祖宗的智慧，我還是不要以褻瀆的言論妄加推翻，否則這個國家就完了。所以呢各位，就容我再強調一次吧：馬利已經像門釘一樣死僵了。

施顧己知道他死了嗎？當然知道。怎麼可能不知道呢？施顧己和他早已不知合夥了多少年。施顧己是他唯一的遺囑執行人、他唯一的遺產管理人、他唯一的遺產受讓人、他唯一的餘產承受人、他唯一的朋友，也是唯一為他送葬的人。不過，施顧己並未因這椿不幸而悲傷過度，出殯當天他依然秉著他傑出商人的本色，辦了一場花費低得不能再低的葬禮。

提起馬利的葬禮，我又想起了一開始說的那句話：馬利確然無疑是死了。各位必須確實了解這一點，否則我接下來要說的故事便毫無精彩奇特之處。就像我們看《哈姆雷特》之前若非百分之百確信哈姆雷特的父親已經死了，那麼他在某個吹著東風的夜裡，到他自己的城牆上遊蕩，根本不足為奇，充其量也不過就是個中年男子在入夜之後，貿貿然出現在一個微風輕拂的地方——比方說像聖保羅墓園這類的地方——只為了嚇嚇他兒子那顆脆弱的心。

施顧己一直沒有塗掉老馬利的名字。幾年過後，商號大門上頭還是寫著：施顧己與馬利。大家都稱這家商號為「施顧己與馬利」。有些生意場上的新手叫施顧己為施顧己，有些則叫他馬利，但無論怎麼稱呼他都會答應：對他來說都一樣。

施顧己呀！是個推磨高手[2]，手底下拿捏得可緊了。他又擠、又摔、又

抓、又摳、又削的，十足一個貪得無厭的老渾球！他的心腸又冷又硬像塊打

火石，就算用鋼棒也擦不出什麼火花來；他也像牡蠣一樣沉默、封閉而孤

僻。他內在的那股子寒意不但使得他老化的五官顯

得更尖銳，臉頰更為皺縮，步伐更遲滯，也使得他眼珠泛血絲，薄薄的嘴唇

發青，甚至還清清楚楚地從他粗嘎的聲音中流洩出來。他的頭頂上、眉毛

上，與尖細的下巴，全都覆著一層冷冷的白霜。他所到之處也總是受他體內

那股低溫感染；熱天裡的辦公室像冰封一樣，到了聖誕節還是連一度也沒暖

上。

外界的冷熱對施顧己幾乎毫無影響。溫熱天他不覺得暖，寒涼天他也不

感到冷。沒有哪一陣風比他更嚴酷，沒有哪一場降雪比他執著，也沒有哪一

場暴雨比他更不容情。惡劣的氣候根本擊不倒他。再猛烈的雨雪雹霰也都只

強得過他一點，那就是雨雪經常是「慷慨地」傾盆而下，施顧己則從來辦不

到。

走在街上，沒有人會歡歡喜喜地與他寒暄：「親愛的施顧己，你好嗎？

什麼時候到我家來坐坐？」沒有乞丐會求他施捨個一文半錢，沒有小孩會向

他詢問時間，而不論男女，這輩子也從來沒有人向施顧己問過路。甚至就連導盲犬都似乎認得他，每當見他迎面走來，便會強拉著主人轉進中庭、巷弄裡，然後搖著尾巴彷彿在說：「失明的主人呀，那種邪惡的眼睛，有還不如沒有！」

不過施顧己又哪在乎呢？這恰是他唯一的樂事。對施顧己而言，循著擁擠的人生道路前進，並一路警告富有惻隱之心的人別靠近，這樣的心情豈不「妙哉」！

有一天──那是一年之中眾多美好日子的其中一天，也就是聖誕前夕──老施顧己正坐在辦公室裡忙著處理帳目。那日裡天寒地凍的，冷風刺骨，還起了濃霧，他聽見外頭巷道裡有人氣喘吁吁地走來走去，為了取暖還一面手拍著胸脯、腳踝著地面的石板。城裡鐘樓的大鐘才敲過三點，但天已經挺黑的了：其實一整天的天色都不太亮，鄰近辦公室的窗裡有燭光搖曳，倒像是在這片彷彿可以觸摸得到的褐色空氣中多了幾處紅色的污漬似的。霧從每一個縫隙和鑰匙孔湧了進來，外頭更是濃霧密布，儘管院子只有一丁點大小，對屋看起來還是縹縹緲緲。眼看髒兮兮的雲霧降下來遮住一切事物，難免讓人懷疑造物者是否就在附近釀造著大霧[3]。

施顧己讓辦公室的門開著，以便監督他的夥計，這名夥計正在後面一個陰陰暗暗、像個油槽似的小房間裡抄寫信件。施顧己房裡只生著小小的火，但夥計房裡的火卻更小得可憐，簡直就像是一塊木炭擺在那裡。不過他不能添煤，因為施顧己將煤炭箱擺在他的房裡，每回只要夥計拿著鏟子走進來，老闆就會說「恐怕是不得不讓你走了」。因此夥計只能圍上白色的羊毛圍巾，企圖就著蠟燭取暖，可惜他想像力不夠豐富，一番努力終告失敗。

「聖誕快樂，舅舅！願上帝保佑你！」一個開朗歡樂的聲音大喊道。那是施顧己的外甥，他以迅雷不及掩耳的速度走進來，一出聲招呼就說了這句話。

「哼！」施顧己說：「鬼扯淡！」

施顧己的外甥在寒霧裡快步走來，走得全身發熱，臉蛋紅潤潤的，眼中閃著光芒，吞吐的氣息也還冒著白煙。

「舅舅，聖誕節是鬼扯淡？」施顧己的外甥說：「我知道你一定不是這個意思。」

「我就是這個意思。」施顧己說：「還聖誕快樂呢！你有什麼權利快樂？你有什麼理由快樂？你都夠窮的了。」

「好啦，」外甥愉快地回答道：「那麼你有什麼權利憂鬱？你有什麼理由不快樂？你都夠有錢的了。」

施顧己一時答不上來，便又「哼！」了一聲，然後又接著一句「鬼扯淡」。

「別生氣了，舅舅。」外甥說。

「叫我怎麼能不生氣？」施顧己反駁道：「誰讓我生在這麼一個充滿蠢人的世界？聖誕快樂！我呸你個聖誕快樂！聖誕節對你有什麼意義？這個時候一到你只會發現自己又得付帳卻口袋空空；發現自己又老了一歲，卻從來沒有多賺一點錢；發現該結帳了，帳本裡整整十二個月的帳目卻條條都是負債。要我說呀，」施顧己憤憤地說：「那些不時把『聖誕快樂』掛在嘴邊的笨蛋，都應該和他們的布丁一起丟到鍋子裡頭煮，再在他們的心口插一支冬青木然後埋掉。就該這樣！」

「舅舅呀！」外甥哀求道。

「甥兒！」施顧己嚴厲應道：「你儘管去過你的聖誕節，也讓我過我自己的聖誕吧。」

「過聖誕！」施顧己的外甥重覆說了一遍：「可是你又不過節。」

「那就讓我不過節吧。」施顧己說：「但願過節對你大有好處！而且是前所未有的好處！」

外甥回答道：「過聖誕便是如此。每當聖誕一來臨，就算不去考慮它那神聖的名稱與來源所得到的崇敬——儘管與聖誕有關的一切都脫離不了這份崇敬——我也總會將它當成一個好節日：一個充滿善意、寬恕、慈悲與愉悅的日子。據我所知，在漫長的一年當中，似乎也只有在這一天男男女女才會不約而同地敞開封閉的心，並且真心地將那些身分卑微的人視為陪伴自己步向人生旅途終點的伴侶，而不是各自奔向不同前程的異類。所以呢，舅舅，雖然聖誕節沒有在我口袋裡添進一丁點的金絲或銀屑，但我相信我的確獲得了好處，以後也還會有好處的；所以我要說：聖誕萬歲！」

油槽間裡的夥計不由自主地鼓起掌來，但他馬上意識到此舉不妥，便連忙撥了撥火，結果把最後僅餘的微弱火星給弄熄了，再也燒不起來。

「再讓我聽到你一點聲響，」施顧己說：「你就準備捲鋪蓋回去過你的聖誕。」然後他轉向外甥又接著說：「這位先生，你倒是挺能言善道的，怎麼不去當議員呢[4]？」

「別生氣，舅舅。好啦！明天到家裡來吃飯吧。」

施顧己說他寧可看著他去……不錯，他的確說絕了，說他寧可看著外甥陷入「那種絕境」，也絕不去吃飯。

「這是為什麼？」施顧己的外甥喊道：「為什麼呢？」

「你為什麼結婚？」施顧己說。

「因為我戀愛了。」

「因為你戀愛了！」施顧己咆哮道，彷彿這是世界上唯一比「聖誕快樂」還要荒謬的事。「再見！」

「可是舅舅，我結婚以前你也從來沒有找過我，現在又何必拿這個當藉口呢？」

「再見。」施顧己說。

「我既不圖你什麼，也不求你什麼，為什麼我們不能好好相處？」

「再見。」施顧己說。

「你這麼堅持，我真的是打心底難過。我們從來沒有起過口角，至少我沒有和你吵過，但這回我這麼做是為了聖誕節的緣故。我還是會繼續保持我過節的愉快心情，那麼就祝你聖誕快樂了，舅舅！」

「再見！」施顧己說。

「也祝你新年快樂！」

「再見！」施顧己說。

然而他的外甥卻一句不滿的話也沒說便走出辦公室。走到外間的門邊，他停下來向舅舅的夥計祝賀聖誕快樂，這名夥計雖然很冷，卻比施顧己熱情，因為他誠心誠意地還了禮。

「又多了個傢伙，」施顧己無意間聽到夥計的話，便喃喃自語：「我這個夥計一個禮拜賺十五先令，還有妻小要養，竟然也說什麼聖誕快樂。我真該進瘋人院去了。」

門外這個瘋子剛送走施顧己的外甥，便迎進了另外兩個人。這兩位身材高大的先生，外表看來和藹可親，他們被請進施顧己的辦公室後，脫下了帽子。他們手裡抱著一些冊子和文件，向他行了個禮。

「施顧己與馬利商號，是吧？」其中一人看了看名冊說：「我能否與施顧己先生，或是馬利先生談談呢？」

「馬利先生已經死了七年。」施顧己回答道：「他就在七年前的這個晚上去世的。」

「我們相信他那位尚在人世的合夥人，一定也和他一樣慷慨。」那人一面說，一面遞出了他的證明文件。

當然了，因為他們是同一類的人。一聽到「慷慨」這不祥的字眼，施顧己不禁皺起眉頭，然後搖搖頭將證明文件又遞了回去。

「施顧己先生，在這個充滿喜氣的年節裡，」那人拿起一枝筆說道：「我們比平時更應該為那些窮苦人家稍盡棉薄之力，因為他們這個時候過得特別辛苦。有成千上萬的人連基本的必需品都沒有，還有幾十萬的人無法過最起碼的舒服日子呀，先生。」

「現在沒有監獄了嗎[5]？」施顧己問。

「監獄多的很哪。」那人又將筆放了下來。

「教區間的聯合救濟院呢?」施顧己問:「還繼續辦嗎?」

「是的。」那人回答道:「不過,我倒希望我能說救濟院已經不存在了。」

「那麼,踏車的刑罰和貧民救濟法也都還照例執行吧?」施顧己說。

「一刻也不停。」

「噢!你剛才的話本來還讓我很擔心,以為發生了什麼事使得這些利民的政策不得不停擺。」施顧己說:「現在聽你這麼說我很高興。」

「但我們幾個人覺得,」那人又說道:「所以我們努力地想籌一點錢,替窮人們買這些政策幾乎並未讓世人在心理與身體上體驗到基督的滿足愉悅,些肉和酒,以及保暖的衣物。我們之所以選擇這個時間,是因為此時窮人的需求十分急迫,而富足的人也樂於慷慨解囊。我該為你登記多少呢?」

「什麼也別寫!」施顧己應道。

「你希望以匿名的方式?」

「我希望再也沒有人來煩我。」施顧己說:「二位,既然你們問我有什麼希望，我就老實說了。我自己不在聖誕節吃喝玩樂，我也不想花錢讓那些懶惰蟲吃喝玩樂。我捐錢贊助我剛才提到的那幾個組織，花得錢也夠多的了，那些生活困苦的人就該到那兒去。」

「可是很多人進不去，還有很多人寧可死也不去。」

「如果他們寧可死，」施顧己說：「那還是死了的好，還可以減少過剩的人口。而且——很抱歉——這些事我一概不知。」

「但你應該知道的。」那人說道。

「那與我無關。」施顧己應道：「一個人管好自己的事就夠了，不用插手別人的閒事，更何況我自己的事都已經忙不過來。再見了，二位！」

那兩位先生心下明白多說無益，便離開了。施顧己重新埋首工作，此時他不但對自己的表現感到十分滿意，心情也比平時輕鬆許多。

此時霧氣更濃，天色也更暗，不少人點起火把走在馬車前頭，替車夫照明引路，也好掙點錢。一旁有座教堂，那已然聲嘶力竭的老鐘，總是從一扇崁在牆上的哥德式窗口偷偷地往下覷著施顧己，而此時卻連教堂的古老鐘樓也瞧不見了，只聽得鐘聲每時每刻在雲霧中響起，後頭還拉著微微的顫音，彷彿兩排牙齒在凍僵的頭顯裡格格打顫。天氣越來越冷。在大街上院子的轉角處，有幾個工人在修煤氣管，生起了好大的一盆火，火盆旁邊圍著一群衣衫襤褸的大人與小孩，正欣喜地對著火烤手，還直眨眼。消防栓被孤立在一旁，溢流的水帶著一股對人類的不滿，鬱鬱地凝結成了冰。商店燈火通明，櫥窗裡燈光的熱度使得冬青的細枝與漿果劈啪作響，也映紅了每個過往行人的蒼白臉孔。

賣雞鴨和雜貨的店鋪生意好得不得了，顧客大排長龍，幾乎叫人不敢相信這時候哪還需要討價還價和賤價拍賣等等無聊的促銷手法。住在警衛森嚴、氣派恢弘的官邸中的市長，也下令五十名廚子、管家，要把聖誕節辦出市長官邸該有的派頭。就連上個禮拜一因為酒醉在街上鬧事而被罰五先令的小裁縫，也在自家的閣樓頂上攪拌著明天要吃的布丁，而他瘦弱的妻子則帶著襁褓中的幼兒出門買牛肉去了。

霧更濃，天更冷了！錐心刺骨的嚴寒。假如當初善良的聖鄧斯坦大主教用這種氣候的些許力道去夾魔鬼的鼻子[6]，而非他平時慣用的武器，魔鬼一定也會痛得呼天搶地。饑腸轆轆的寒冷像狗啃骨頭似的囓咬著一個小孩細小的鼻子，只見他俯身往施顧己門上的鑰匙孔一湊，便大聲唱起聖誕頌歌：

願你無憂無慮，愉快的先生！

上帝保佑你，

才唱了這麼一句，施顧己便氣沖沖地抓起直尺，嚇得報佳音的人拔腿就跑，鑰匙孔四周只剩一片濃霧，說得更確切一點，是一片寒霜。

下班的時間終於到了。施顧己心不甘情不願從椅凳上站起來，默默地向待在油槽間裡、滿心期待的夥計示意可以走了，夥計見狀立刻吹熄蠟燭，戴上帽子。

「你明天想放一整天假，是吧？」施顧己問。

「是的，老闆，如果方便的話。」

「不方便。」施顧己說：「也不公平。如果我扣你半克朗（即兩個半先令）的薪水，你一定會覺得我虧待你，對不對？」

夥計無力地笑笑。

「可是，」施顧己說：「你放假一天我薪水照付，你卻不覺得我很吃虧。」

夥計說一年也不過就這麼一次。

「每年十二月二十五日就可以趁機扒人口袋裡的錢，根本說不過去！」施顧己把大衣的鈕扣一路扣到頂，一面又說：「不過，明天還是讓你放一天假吧。後天早上記得早點來！」

夥計答應後，施顧己便嘟噥著走了出去。一轉眼辦公室關上了，夥計繫上白色圍巾，長長的兩端垂在腰際（因為他沒有大衣）。他跟在一群小男孩後面，沿著斜斜的康希爾街滑行，滑了二十幾回以慶祝聖誕夜，然後才以最快的速度衝回坎登鎮，準備回家玩捉迷藏。

施顧己在他經常光顧的那家冷清清的小飯館裡，吃了一頓冷清清的晚餐；他讀遍所有的報紙，又拿出存摺排遣夜晚剩餘的時間之後，才回家睡覺。他住的公寓是已過世的合夥人生前的住處，一棟陰陰暗暗的建築，裡頭幾間暗無天日的房間，怎麼會就這麼杵在這條死胡同裡，叫人無論如何也想不通，不免要懷疑它是否在年輕時和其他房子玩躲貓貓，結果跑到這裡頭來便再也找不著出路。如今它也夠老、夠荒涼的，因為只有施顧己一人住在這裡，其他房間則都出租作為辦公室。院子裡烏漆抹黑的，就連對這裡瞭若指掌的施顧己也得伸手摸索著。霧與霜凝在房子又黑又舊的大門四周，彷彿天候的精靈正哀戚地坐在門前沉思。

其實說句實在話，門上的門環除了奇大無比之外，倒也沒什麼特別之處。再說句實在話，打施顧己住進這個地方開始，早晚都瞧得見門環，而且施顧己和倫敦城裡的任何人一樣──說得大膽一點，甚至包括整個市議會，所有的市議員和同業公會會員在內──毫無所謂的想像力。還有一點要提醒諸位的，自從當天下午他最後一次提起他那死了七年的合夥人馬利之後，腦子裡便再也沒有想起過他。那麼請問有誰能向我解釋一下，當施顧己將鑰匙插進門鎖時，為什麼在門上看見的竟忽然不再是門環，而無緣無故變成了馬利的臉呢？

馬利的臉。它可不像院子裡其他東西一樣昏暗模糊，而是有一道黯淡的光環繞著，像是陰暗地窖裡一隻腐爛的龍蝦閃著磷光。臉上並不顯得憤怒或兇暴，只是用馬利平時的目光看著施顧己：幽靈般的眼鏡往上翻，靠在幽靈般的額頭上，頭髮亂得有點奇怪，好像是被一股氣息或熱氣給吹亂的。雖然眼睛睜得老大，卻是眨也不眨，再加上死灰般的臉色，使得這張臉更顯得恐怖。不過這種恐怖的感覺卻似乎和臉本身的表情無關，而是外界一種不受制於這張臉的氛圍。

施顧已正待定睛細看，臉卻又成了門環。

要說他不吃驚，或說他沒有感覺到從小便不曾有過的毛骨悚然，那是騙人的。但他還是重新捏住鑰匙，穩穩地開了鎖，走進去，點燃蠟燭。

關上門之前，他確實頓了一下，有點遲疑；他也確實先仔細地檢查門後，似乎擔心馬利的髮辮會突然往前廳裡翹出來嚇他。不過門後除了釘著門環的螺釘和螺帽之外，什麼也沒有；於是他「呸！」了兩聲，然後砰地把門關上。

關門聲像雷鳴似的在屋裡不停回響。樓上的每個房間，和樓下地窖裡的每只酒桶，好像都各自發出了回音。施顧已可不是一個會被回音嚇著的人，他將門鎖牢，穿過前廳走上樓梯，一面慢慢地走一面剪著燭花。

你大可以信口開河說有人駕著六駕馬車駛上了一段老舊的樓梯，或者是從一條剛剛通過卻滿是紙漏的議會法案的大漏洞中駛了過來，但我得說把一輛靈柩車弄上這段樓梯倒不是不可能的事，而且就算橫著上，讓車前橫木對著牆壁，後門向著樓梯欄杆，也同樣輕而易舉。寬不但是夠寬，還綽綽有餘；也許正因為如此，施顧己才會覺得昏暗的前頭，好像有一輛靈柩車開上樓去。此時就算點燃街邊的六盞煤氣燈，也照不亮這個樓梯口，所以你應該可以想見施顧己只點著那蠅頭燭火，四周有多暗了。

施顧己繼續往上爬，一點也不在乎：黑暗不用花什麼錢，施顧己喜歡得很。但在關上厚重的房門之前，他又到各個房間巡視了一下；因為他想起了剛才那張臉，所以覺得有必要這麼做。

客廳、臥室、雜物間，一切如常。桌子底下沒有人，沙發底下沒有人，壁爐裡頭小小的火，湯匙和盤子已備妥，壁爐邊架上還有一小鍋麥片粥（施顧己有點鼻塞）。床底下沒有人，衣櫥裡沒有人，他掛在牆上的睡袍樣子有點可疑，但裡面也沒有人。雜物間和往常沒有兩樣。同樣的爐柵，同樣的鞋子，依然是兩只魚簍，一個三腳的臉盆架，和一把火鉗。

他十分滿意地關上了門，把自己鎖在房內，而且還上了兩道鎖，平常他並沒有這個習慣。確定不會再受到驚嚇了，他這才脫掉領結，穿上睡袍和拖鞋，戴上睡帽，然後坐到爐火前吃起了麥片粥。

火的確非常微弱，在這麼寒冷的夜裡幾乎起不了作用。他不得不靠近一點，身子稍微往前傾，才能從這一丁點的炭塊當中感受到一絲暖意。壁爐已然老舊，那是很久以前某個荷蘭的商人建造的，壁爐四周都鋪著古老的荷蘭瓷磚，上頭畫了一些聖經的故事。有該隱和亞伯一家人，有法老的女兒、示巴女王、從羽絨墊般的雲端降落的天使、亞伯拉罕一家、伯沙撒一家、搭著奶油碟出海的使徒 7，還有數以百計的人物足以吸引他的注意力；然而馬利，已經死了七年的馬利的臉，卻有如古代先知的杖 8 一般將一切都吞噬了。假如每塊磚起先都是空白，而且又能憑著感應，將施顧已片片段段的思緒顯現出來，那麼浮現在每一塊磚上的必定都是老馬利的面孔。

「鬼扯淡！」施顧已說著便在房裡踱起步來。

來回走了幾次以後，他又坐了下來。當他把頭往椅背上靠去，無意間瞄見一個掛在房中，已經廢棄不用的搖鈴，這個搖鈴與頂樓的某個房間相通，至於當初設置的原因則早已記不得了。這時他忽然感到無比驚訝，還有一種怪異不可解的恐懼，因為他看到搖鈴竟然開始搖晃起來。一開始搖得很輕很輕，幾乎沒有發出聲音，但不久便鈴聲大作，而房子裡的每個鈴也都跟著叮咚作響。

鈴聲大概響了半分鐘，又或是一分鐘，但卻像有一小時那麼久。鈴聲同時響起，也同時停止。隨後，樓底深處又傳來匡啷匡啷的聲音，好像有人在酒商地窖的木桶上，拖一條沉重的鐵鍊似的。施顧己忽然想起曾聽人說過，鬼屋裡的鬼據說都拖著鐵鍊。

地窖的門突然轟然一聲開了，接著他聽見噪音越來越大聲，就在樓下，然後走上了樓梯，然後直接便朝他的房門而來。

「鬼扯淡！」施顧己說：「我才不信。」

然而當它毫不遲疑地穿過厚重的房門，進入房裡出現在他眼前時，他還是變了臉色。而且就在它進門的時候，奄奄一息的火焰倏地竄高起來，彷彿喊了一聲：「我認得他！是馬利的鬼魂！」接著便又黯淡下來。

同一張臉，就是那張臉。馬利留著髮辮，穿著平日的背心、緊身褲和靴子；靴筒上的流蘇也和他的髮辮、他上衣的衣裾、他頂上的頭髮一樣豎直起來。他拖著的鐵鍊緊緊地扣在腰間。長長的鐵鍊像尾巴似的纏繞著他，而且是以錢櫃、鑰匙、大鎖、帳本、契約以及鋼鐵精製的錢包製成的（施顧己仔細地瞧過了）。他的身子透明，因此施顧己看著他時，可以看穿他的背心並瞧見他大衣背後的兩個鈕扣。

施顧己以前經常聽人說馬利沒心沒肝，但直到現在他才真正相信。

不，即使到了現在他也還是不信。儘管他將鬼魂徹頭徹尾地看個仔細，見到它就站在自己跟前；儘管他感覺到了鬼魂那雙冰冷無神的眼睛所透射出來的寒意；也儘管他發現鬼魂的頭與下巴纏著一條他從未見過的頭巾，也留意到了那條頭巾的質地⋯他卻依然不肯輕信，而且極力想否決自己的感覺。

「這是怎麼啦！」施顧己的口氣冷漠嚴苛地一如往常：「你找我有什麼事？」

「可多了！」——是馬利的聲音，毋庸置疑。

「你是誰？」

「你該問我從前是誰。」

「好吧，你從前是誰？」施顧己提高了嗓音說：「做鬼還這麼挑剔。」他本來想說「愛作怪……」，但還是改了口，覺得這樣比較恰當。

「在世的時候我是你的合夥人雅各・馬利。」

「你能不能……你能不能坐下？」施顧己滿臉狐疑地看著他，問道。

「可以。」

「那就坐下吧。」

施顧己這麼問是因為他不知道全身如此透明的鬼魂可不可能坐到椅子上，他心想萬一它不能坐，可能還得尷尬地做一番解釋。不過鬼魂卻面對著壁爐坐了下來，彷彿對這個動作已經習以為常。

「你不相信我是真的。」鬼魂說。

「我是不信。」施顧己說。

「除了你的感覺之外，你還需要什麼證據來證明我的真實性？」

「我不知道。」施顧己說。

「你為什麼懷疑自己的感覺？」

「因為只要小小的一件事就能影響感覺。」施顧己說：「胃稍微不舒服就會產生幻覺。你可能只是一小塊沒有消化掉的牛肉、一坨芥末醬、一小片乾酪、一口半生不熟的馬鈴薯。不管你是什麼東西，要說你是墳裡的鬼，還不如說是粉做的粿！」

施顧己一向不太喜歡開玩笑，而此時在他心裡也沒有開玩笑的念頭。事實上他只是想藉著說說俏皮話轉移自己的注意力，壓制內心的恐懼，因為幽靈的聲音已經讓他寒到骨子裡去了。

這麼靜靜坐著，直盯那雙目不轉睛又呆滯的眼睛看上一會，施顧己立刻感到坐立不安。還有一件很恐怖的事，那就是鬼魂本身也散發著地獄般的氣氛。施顧己自己倒沒什麼感覺，只是事實擺在眼前；因為鬼魂雖然坐著一動也不動，它的頭髮、衣裾、流蘇卻像是被爐子的熱氣吹得晃動不止。

「你看到這根牙籤了嗎？」施顧己再次出擊，為的還是剛才提到的原因，哪怕只是一瞬間，他還是希望能轉移鬼魂凝視自己的目光。

「看到了。」鬼魂說。

「你並沒有看著牙籤啊。」施顧己說。

「不過我還是看到了。」鬼魂說。

「好啦！」施顧己回說：「我要是還繼續吞忍下去，下半輩子就少不了被一大群我自己幻想出來的小妖精折磨。鬼扯淡，我告訴你……鬼扯淡！」

他一說完，幽靈忽然發出可怕的叫聲，並不斷搖晃鐵鍊，那聲響又淒慘又駭人，嚇得施顧已緊抓住椅子以免昏厥過去。但是接下來的情景卻更是叫他魂飛魄散，只見鬼魂像是在屋裡熱得受不了，便解下纏在頭上的布條，就在這一瞬間它的下巴竟掉落到胸前！

施顧已不禁跪倒在地，雙手將臉搗住。

「天哪！」他說：「可怕的幽靈啊，你為什麼要這樣嚇我？」

「你這凡夫俗子！」鬼魂應道：「你現在相信我的存在了嗎？」

「相信了。」施顧已說：「我不得不信。但為什麼亡靈會在人世間遊蕩，又為什麼找上我？」

「因為每個人內在的靈魂，」鬼魂回答道：「都必須走向人群，到處遊走，假如在世時靈魂沒有離開，死後也躲不掉。靈魂註定要在世間遊蕩——真是可憐呀！——註定要親眼瞧瞧它已經無福消受的一切，這一切原本是它在世時可以與人分享的幸福來源！」

幽靈又號叫了一聲，晃動鐵鍊，並悲痛地扭絞著虛幻的雙手。

「告訴我，」施顧己顫抖著聲音問道：「你為什麼被鏈住？」

「我身上的鐵鍊是我在世時打造的。」鬼魂回答：「這是我親手一個環節、一寸一寸接起來的，我心甘情願地纏著它，也心甘情願地拖著它。它的樣式你難道不覺得熟悉嗎？」

施顧己越來越抖得厲害。

「或許你也想知道，」鬼魂接著說：「你自己身上所纏繞著的那條粗粗的鐵鍊有多重、多長吧？在七年前的聖誕夜，剛好就跟我這條鍊子一樣重、一樣長。但後來你又加緊努力，現在可是沉甸甸的一條鐵鍊了！」

施顧己往四周的地板覷了一眼，本以為會看見身旁圍繞著百來公尺的鋼索，但卻是什麼也沒看見。

「雅各，」他哀求道：「老雅各‧馬利，再多說一點。跟我說幾句安慰的話吧，雅各。」

「我沒有安慰的話可說。」鬼魂應道：「艾布內茲‧施顧己，安慰的話來自另一個領域，只能由另一種使者傳遞給另一類的人。而且我也不能暢所欲言，我只能再多說那麼一點點。我不能休息，我不能停留，我不能在任何地方流連。從前我的靈魂從來沒有離開過我們的辦公室——你可得聽仔細了！——終其一生，我的靈魂都沒有飄出過我們這窄小的錢坑，前頭還有辛苦漫長的旅程等著我呢！」

施顧己有個習慣，每回他沉思的時候便會將手插進褲袋裡。此時他細細想著鬼魂的話，手不由自主便又插進口袋，但他既沒有抬起眼皮，也沒有站起身來。

「你一定是動作太慢了，雅各。」施顧己以一種實事求是的態度說道，但口氣中卻帶著謙卑與恭謹。

「動作慢！」鬼魂重覆著他的話。

「都死了七年了，」施顧己若有所思地說：「你一直都在四處奔波？」

「時時刻刻，」鬼魂說：「不得休息，不得安寧，不斷受著良心的譴責。」

「你移動的速度快嗎？」施顧己說。

「乘風飛行。」鬼魂回道。

「七年之間你應該跑了不少地方。」施顧己說。

鬼魂一聽又慘叫一聲，還用力晃動鐵鍊，匡啷匡啷的巨響在死寂的夜裡聽來尤其令人心驚，讓守夜人聽到絕對會以擾亂安寧的罪名將它逮捕。

「呵！被俘虜、被束縛、被層層的鐵鍊困住，」鬼魂咆哮道：「根本不知道不朽的人物已經不停努力了千百年，因為要發揮地球上一切可能的良善，需要的是永恆的時間。也不知道每一個基督徒的靈魂在小小的範圍中行善，無論是什麼樣的範圍，他們都會覺得行善的方式太多而人生卻又太短。更不知道再多的悔恨也彌補不了一生中錯失的機會！唉！我就是這樣！而我就是這樣！」

「可是雅各，你一直都是做生意的好手呀。」施顧已顫抖著糾正道，他已經開始把整個情況套到自己身上來了。

「生意！」鬼魂又扭絞著手喊道：「人類是我的生意。眾人的福祉是我的生意；慈悲、憐憫、寬恕與博愛都是我的生意。在我包羅萬象的生意當中，那些交易買賣只不過是滄海一粟！」

鬼魂伸手舉起鐵鍊，又重重地往地板一摔，彷彿它一切徒然的悲苦都是這鐵鍊所造成的。

「在時光流轉的一年當中，」幽靈說：「這個時候最令我痛苦。為什麼我以前走在人群裡總是雙眼低垂，為什麼我從不曾抬起頭來，看看引領三王前往某個貧窮居所的那顆明星呢，？難道我身旁就沒有窮人家可以讓星光指引我前往的嗎？」

聽著鬼魂這樣說下去，施顧己感到非常驚惶，身子也開始抖得厲害。

「你聽我說！」鬼魂喊道：「我的時間已經不多。」

「我會的，」施顧己說：「但不要對我太嚴苛！別再說那些不著邊際的話了，雅各！求求你！」

「我是怎麼在你眼前現形的，我也不清楚。不過我已經在你身邊坐了好些日子，只不過你看不見而已。」

這可不是什麼舒坦的畫面。施顧己一面顫抖，一面揩去眉毛上的汗水。

「我的懲罰並不輕。」鬼魂繼續說道：「我今晚是來警告你的，你還有機會，也還有希望避免步入我的後塵。艾布內茲，這是我為你爭取來的機會與希望。」

「你一向都是我的好友，謝謝！」施顧己說。

「接下來會有三個精靈來找你。」鬼魂又說。

施顧己的臉拉得好長，幾乎就和鬼魂剛才下巴掉下來一個模樣。他抖著聲音問道：

「這就是你所說的機會和希望嗎，雅各？」

「是的。」

「我……我想我寧可不要。」施顧己說。

「如果它們不來找你，」鬼魂說：「你就不可能不重蹈我的覆轍。明天當一點的鐘聲響起，就是第一個精靈要出現了。」

「它們三個就不能同時來，一次解決嗎，雅各？」施顧己暗示著說。

「第二個精靈會在第二天夜裡同一個時間出現。第三個則會在第三天夜裡十二點的鐘聲敲完最後一響的時候出現。別指望再見到我了；還有，為了你自己好，你要記得我們之間發生過的事！」

鬼魂說完這些話之後，從桌上拿起布條，又重新纏回頭上。施顧己之所以知道，是因為它用布條將下巴拉攏時，牙齒發出了猛烈的撞擊聲。他再度大著膽子抬起頭來，發現那位靈異訪客正直挺挺地面對著自己，鐵鍊則一圈圈地纏在手臂上。

鬼魂倒退著離去，每走一步，窗戶便自動打開一些，因此當它到達窗邊時，窗子已然大敞。它示意施顧己上前，施顧己便照做了。就在他們相距兩步之處，馬利的鬼魂舉起手來，阻止他再往前，施顧己便停了下來。

與其說他是服從，倒不如說是訝異與恐懼所致：因為鬼魂的手一舉起，他便感覺到空中響起了嘈嘈切切的雜音，有斷續的悔恨、慟哭聲，有無比悲戚與自責的嗚咽。鬼魂傾聽一陣之後，也跟著加入戚然哀歌的行列，然後便向外飄進了淒寒的黑夜。

施顧己由於好奇心驅使，也顧不得害怕便跟著到了窗邊，往外看去。

空中全是幽靈，匆匆忙忙地飄來飄去，一面還發出悲痛的呻吟。每個幽靈都跟馬利的鬼魂一樣套著鎖鏈，有一些人被綁在一起（可能是犯了罪的政府官員），沒有一個是自由之身。不少幽靈在世時都與施顧己相識，其中一個穿著白色背心的老鬼魂與他尤其熟，它的腳踝上綁著一個巨大無比的鐵製保險櫃，嘴裡哀號不已，因為它看到底下某扇門前有個懷抱幼兒的不幸母親，卻無法向她伸出援手。所有幽靈的痛苦顯然都是因為它們企圖為人類做點善事，卻永遠也辦不到了。

最後是這些鬼魅隱進了霧中，或是濃霧將它們包圍？他也看不明白。總之它們和它們那靈幻的聲音是一起消失了，黑夜又恢復了他剛才回家時的模樣。

施顧己關上窗子，檢查了一下鬼魂進入的那扇門。門上的兩道鎖還是和他親手上鎖時一樣鎖得牢牢的，門閂也毫無異狀。他想說「鬼扯淡！」，但才說一個字便住口了。或許是剛才情緒過於激動，或許是一整天的疲累，或許是幽冥世界的驚鴻一瞥，或許是與鬼魂那段冗長的談話，也或許是時間太晚了，他實在需要休息。於是他直奔床頭，也沒有寬衣，倒頭便呼呼大睡起來。

註：

1. 馬利已經像門釘一樣死僵了——原文為「Old Marley was as dead as a door-nail.」。

2. 聖誕頌歌（A Christmas Carol）中的主角施顧己（Scrooge），是個自私自利的商人。而狄更斯小說藝術的成就之一，是賦予了小說人物姓名上的特殊意義；「scrooge」含有吝嗇鬼、守財奴的意思。

3. 施顧己的辦公室位在倫敦商業中心西堤區的正中央。維多利亞時代的倫敦市，是狄更斯（Charles Dickens, 1812—1870）所熟悉的大都市，當時的倫敦由於工業革命而使用煤炭，經常瀰漫著濃霧，倫敦從此有「霧都」之名。

4. 一八三一年，狄更斯成為《議會鏡報》的新聞記者，必須以速記的方式謄寫國會議員的演說詞，所以非常熟悉說話的藝術。

5. 依照當時的法律，許多人因無法償還債務而入獄。狄更斯的父親曾經因為債務問題，於一八二四年時被囚禁於馬夏爾西（Marshalsea）監獄中數月。

6. 聖鄧斯坦大主教——傳說中，聖鄧斯坦（Saint Dunstan）是一個在北東蘇塞克斯郡（Sussex）裡一個村莊鐵匠鋪工作的鐵匠。一日，魔鬼喬裝成美麗的女人誘惑他，聖鄧斯坦發現魔鬼的詭計，而用熾熱的紅色鐵鉗夾住魔鬼的鼻子。

7. 該隱和亞伯（Cains and Abels）——該隱是《聖經》中亞當和夏娃的長子，亞伯的哥哥。據《創世紀》（4:2）記載，該隱從事務農，亞伯牧羊。該隱後來因為憤怒而殺死亞伯。

——《聖經》記載，摩西（Moses）被一位法老的女兒從尼羅河裡救起來，在

法老的女兒——

埃及法老的王宮裡生活了四十年。

示巴女王（Queens of Sheba）——非洲東部示巴王國的女王。根據《舊約聖經》（列王紀第十章）記載，她因為仰慕當時以色列國王所羅門的才智，不惜紆尊降貴，前往以色列向所羅門提親。

亞伯拉罕（Abraham）——原名亞伯蘭，耶和華賜名為亞伯拉罕，意思是「多國的宗祖」（《創世紀》17:1-8）。神與亞伯拉罕立約，應許他繁盛的後裔、萬族得福。

伯沙撒（Belshazzars）——據《聖經》但以理書記載，新巴比倫王國的末代國王伯沙撒在盛宴上狂歡時，突然出現了一只手指（不具備連接的身體，代表著神的示警）在牆壁上寫下文字：預言了新巴比倫王國的滅亡，伯沙撒僅統治七年，就被波斯帝國攻陷滅亡。

8. 古代先知的杖——Prophet's rod，《聖誕頌歌》含有寓言勸世的意味，「古代先知的杖」，暗喻《出埃及記》中的一幕：亞倫的杖變成了蛇，雖然法老召來術士用邪術如法炮製，但亞倫的杖卻吞噬了他們的杖。

9. 這裡的「三王」，指「東方三博士」（Magi, Three Wise Men）。據馬太福音記載，耶穌出生時，三博士在東方看見往伯利恆方向的天空上，有一顆明亮的星星，在這顆星星的指引下，來到耶穌的出生地。

三個精靈中的第一個

施顧已醒來時四下一片漆黑,從床上望出去,幾乎分辨不出哪裡是透光的窗戶,哪裡又是臥房晦暗的牆面。他鼬鼠般的雙眼正努力地想看透黑暗,忽然聽見鄰近的教堂響起了整點的鐘聲。他便聽聽看現在幾點鐘。

大大出乎他意料之外的是沉沉的鐘聲從六響到七響,從七響到八響,規規矩矩地敲了十二下,然後才停止。十二點!他上床的時候都已經兩點。鐘壞了。一定是有冰柱掉進大鐘裡頭去。十二點!

他按下反覆報時鐘的彈簧,想看看那座荒謬的大鐘錯得有多離譜。報時鐘輕快地彈了十二下,然後也停住了。

「怎麼可能?」施顧已說:「我不可能已經睡了一整天又睡上大半夜的。但要說是太陽出了問題,現在是中午十二點也不可能呀!」

這麼一想之後,他不禁不安地爬下床來,摸索著走到窗邊。他先得用睡袍的袖子擦去窗上的霜才看得見外頭，但卻也幾乎看不到什麼。他只能勉強察覺出外頭的霧依然濃密，天也依然凜冽，也沒有人群熙熙攘攘的嘈雜聲，就好像黑夜已經擊退白晝而佔有了世界；要是這樣就太好了，因為若是沒有日子可以數，那麼「見票三日後即支付艾布內茲・施顧己先生⋯⋯」等等的，也不過就是廢紙一張罷了。

施顧己又回到床上，他想了再想，一遍又一遍地想，但就是想不通。他越想越困惑，但越是不願去想，偏偏又想得越吃力。馬利的鬼魂簡直讓他方寸大亂。每當他經過一番深思熟慮，好不容易說服自己那只是一場夢時，他的心卻又會像一條拉緊後鬆開的彈簧一樣，彈回到原點，於是他又得將同樣的問題從頭再思考一遍：「那究竟是不是一場夢？」

施顧己就這麼躺著，直到鐘聲又敲過三刻鐘，他驀然回想起鬼魂的預警：一點的鐘聲響起時將有訪客到來，於是他決定清醒地等待預定的時間過去。更何況他要想入睡恐怕比登天還難，那麼這應該是他此時最明智之舉了。

那一刻鐘好漫長，他不只一次以為自己在不知不覺中打了盹，沒聽到鐘響。就在他側耳傾聽之際，鐘聲終於響了。

「叮噹！」

「一刻鐘。」施顧己數著。

「叮噹！」

「半點鐘！」施顧己說。

「叮噹！」

「三刻鐘。」施顧己說。

「叮噹！」

「整一點。」施顧己得意洋洋地說：「什麼事也沒有！」

他說話時整點鐘聲還沒響，話說完才聽見那深沉、單調、空洞、悶悶的一響。此時房裡立刻大放光明，他的床帷也被拉了開來。

我可告訴你，他的床帷是被一隻手給拉開的。而被拉開來的既不是他腳邊的帳幔，也不是他背後的帳幔，而是他面對著的帳幔。床帷被拉開了，施顧己嚇得斜坐起身來，卻發現自己正和拉開床帷的那個幽靈訪客面對著面，靠得就像我和你這麼近，而我的靈魂現在就站在你身邊。

它的長相很奇特——像個小孩：但要說是像個老頭，這老頭彷彿透過某種靈異媒介出現一般，離得好遠好遠，身形便也縮得有如孩童。纏繞著它的頸子並垂在背上的頭髮似乎因為上了年紀而泛白，但是它臉上卻又沒有一絲皺紋，肌膚更是光滑細緻到了極點。它的腿和腳長得極為纖細，並和上肢一樣赤裸著。它穿著一件潔白的長袍，腰間束著一條色澤美麗的晶亮腰帶。它手裡握著一把鮮綠的冬青，衣服上卻裝飾著夏天的花朵，與象徵嚴冬的冬青恰成強烈對比。不過最奇怪的是它的頭頂上竟迸射出一束明亮而搶眼的光線，所以這一切才能瞭然入目，也或許因為如此，它腋下才會夾著一頂像熄燈器一樣的大帽子，在心情低潮的時候可以蓋在頭上掩去光芒。

然而，當施顧己更仔細地看過它之後，卻發現就連這點也不是它最奇特之處；因為它的腰帶一忽兒這邊閃，一忽兒那邊亮，忽明忽暗，於是幽靈本身也隨著明滅不定：一下子只有一隻手臂，一下子又只有一條腿，一下子卻只有一雙腿沒有頭，一下子又只有頭沒有身子……各個消失的部位都沒入了漆黑之中，全然看不清。但最奇妙的是，它又會恢復原樣，依然那樣地明亮清晰。

「這位先生，」施顧己問道：「事先向我通報要來的幽靈就是你嗎？」

「就是我！」

它的聲音又輕又柔，而且異常地小聲，好像距離很遙遠，並非在他身邊。

「你是誰，你又是做什麼的？」施顧己問道。

「我是過去的聖誕精靈。」

「遙遠的過去？」施顧己見它身材矮小，便這麼問。

「不，是你的過去。」

此刻若有人問施顧己為什麼，他恐怕也說不出個所以然來，不過他真的很想看看精靈戴帽子的模樣，便求它將帽子戴上。

「什麼！」精靈驚呼道：「你難道這麼快就想用世俗的雙手將我散發的光給滅了？拜你和你那些同類的冥頑不靈之賜，才有了這頂帽子，這麼些年來你們逼我戴上帽子，還得將帽沿壓得低低的，這樣還不夠呀！」

施顧己必恭必敬地澄清自己絕無意冒犯，也完全不知道自己這輩子曾經逼迫精靈「戴帽子」。接著他鼓起勇氣問它到這裡來有何貴幹。

「為了你的幸福！」鬼魂說。

施顧己表達了感激之意，卻又不免暗想要是能好好休息一夜不受打擾，應該是比較幸福的事吧。精靈定是聽見了他的心聲，立刻便說：

「那麼，就算是為了導正你吧。注意了！」

它一面說一面伸出強有力的手，輕輕抓住施顧己的胳臂。

「起來！跟我走！」

施顧己真想反駁它說：這種天候、這個時間並不適合散步；說床鋪很溫暖，而溫度計上顯示外頭卻是零下好幾度；說自己雖然穿著衣服，卻只是單薄的拖鞋、睡衣和睡帽；說自己當時還患了感冒。但即使他說了，也沒有用。抓住他的手雖然纖弱猶如女子，卻是令人無法反抗。他起了身，不料精靈竟朝窗戶走去，他立刻摟住它的長袍哀求道：

「我是個凡人，會摔下去的。」

「只要我在這裡摸一下，」幽靈一邊說著，一邊將手放在施顧己的胸口：「你就會得到各種保護了！」

話一說完，他們立刻穿牆而出，站在一條開闊的鄉間道路上，兩旁盡是田野。城市整個消失了，一點痕跡也不留。黑暗與濃霧也跟著消失了，因為眼前是個晴朗、寒冷的冬日，地上還覆蓋著白雪。

「老天啊！」施顧已四下張望，並交握起雙手說：「這裡是我出生的地方。我的童年是在這裡度過的！」

精靈以柔和的眼神望著他。它的手雖然只是瞬間輕輕一碰，老施顧已卻似乎仍然還能感覺到。他感覺到空氣中飄著千百種氣味，而每種氣味都使他聯想起千百種遺忘了許久許久的思緒、希望、歡樂與牽掛！

「你的嘴唇在顫抖，」精靈說：「你的臉頰上又是怎麼回事？」

施顧已以一種不尋常的哽咽聲音，喃喃地說他長了一粒粉刺，然後請求精靈帶他到他想去的地方。

「你還記得路嗎？」精靈問道。

「怎麼不記得？」施顧已激動地大喊：「我閉著眼睛都能走。」

「那你竟然遺忘了這麼多年，真是奇怪！」精靈說：「我們走吧。」

他們沿著路走，路旁的每扇門、每根柱子、每棵樹，施顧已都認得，最後遠遠地看見了一個小市鎮，鎮上有橋、有教堂，還有一條蜿蜒的河。這時有幾匹鬃毛亂蓬蓬的小馬朝他們快步奔來，一旁還有幾輛由農人駕著的輕便馬車與貨車，騎在馬背上的男孩正對著車上的男孩大聲呼喊。這些小男孩各個精神抖擻，互相叫嚷，直到開闊的鄉野間充斥著這歡樂的樂音，連清爽的空氣也聽得開心地笑了。

「這些只是過去的幻影，」精靈說：「他們感覺不到我們的存在。」

愉快的旅人慢慢地接近，到了眼前，施顧已認出了每一個人，還叫得出名字來。為什麼見到他們使他分外欣喜！為什麼當他們經過身旁時，他冷漠的眼睛閃著光芒，心怦怦跳得厲害！為什麼當他看見他們在路口與小岔道分手各自回家，聽見他們互道聖誕快樂時，心中竟充滿了喜悅！聖誕快樂對施顧己有什麼意義？呸你個聖誕快樂！聖誕快樂讓他得到過什麼好處？

「學校裡還有人。」精靈說：「有一個被同伴拋下的小孩，還孤零零地在那裡。」

施顧己說他知道，並開始啜泣起來。

他們離開大路，走上一條施顧己記憶深刻的小徑，不久便來到一棟暗紅磚屋，屋頂上有一個圓頂閣，上頭立著一隻風信雞，裡面則掛了一口鐘。這是一間大宅子，不過顯然已經好景不再，因為寬敞的廚房、洗衣間等等都幾乎棄置不用，潮溼的牆壁上爬滿了青苔，窗子殘破，門也腐朽了。幾隻雞在馬廄裡走來走去，咯咯叫著，馬車房和牲口棚裡全都長滿了雜草。屋裡，也同樣見不到昔日景況。他們走進荒涼的門廳，往許多扇開著的門裡瞄了幾眼，發現每個房間都幾乎沒什麼家俱，冷冷地，空蕩蕩地。空氣裡有股塵土味，整個地方空得淒涼，不知怎地總叫人回想起從前常常點著蠟燭從床上爬下來，卻又常常找不到什麼東西吃的景況。

精靈和施顧已穿過了門廳，走到屋後的一扇門前。門自動開了，現出一個狹長、簡陋又陰暗的房間，加上幾排簡單的冷杉板凳和課桌，更顯得空空蕩蕩。其中一張課桌前坐著一個孤單單的男孩，正靠著微弱的火光看書。施顧已坐到一張板凳上，他早已遺忘自己當年這副可憐的模樣，如今看了，不禁淚眼汪汪。

屋裡潛伏的回聲，壁板後面老鼠吱吱的叫聲與慌亂的奔跑聲，屋後那蕭條的院子裡，半融半凍的排水管傳來的滴水聲，一株死氣沉沉的白楊，風吹拂過光禿枝枒間的颯颯聲，空空的儲藏室門板緩緩晃動的咿呀聲，還有火爐裡的劈啪聲，聲聲都敲進了施顧己的心坎，他心一軟，眼淚更是撲簌簌掉個不停。

精靈碰碰他的手臂，指了指正埋首用功的年少的他。忽然有個人，一副異國的裝束──看起來異常真切──站在窗外，腰間繫著一柄斧頭，還牽了一頭馱著木柴的驢子[1]。

「是阿里巴巴呀！」施顧己欣喜若狂地大喊：「是親愛的老友，好心的阿里巴巴！沒錯，我認得他！有一年聖誕，那個孤零零的小孩獨自一人留在這裡，他的確來過，那是他第一次來，就像這個樣子。可憐的孩子！還有瓦倫泰和他那野蠻的兄弟奧森[2]，他們走過去了！還有那個叫什麼名字的？在睡夢中被人抬到大馬士革的城門口，全身只穿著一條內褲，你沒看到嗎？還有蘇丹的馬夫被妖靈倒掛起來，瞧他頭朝下頂著呢！活該。我高興得很。他憑什麼娶公主[3]！」

要是倫敦生意場上的朋友聽見施顧己如此正經八百、又哭又笑地談論這類話題，又看見他臉上誇張而興奮的表情，一定非常詫異。

「是那隻鸚鵡！」施顧己大叫：「綠色的身體，黃色的尾巴，頭頂上還冒出一簇像萵苣的東西，牠就在那裡！可憐的魯賓遜，他環島一周回來之後，鸚鵡這麼叫著：『可憐的魯賓遜，你上哪兒去了，魯賓遜？』魯賓遜以為自己在作夢，但不是。你知道的，其實是那隻鸚鵡。還有星期五，拚了命地往小海灣逃！加油！跑！快跑[4]！」

接著他以平日極為罕見的快速轉變，一下子自憐自艾起來：「可憐的孩子！」說著又哭了。

「我真希望……」施顧己用袖口抹乾眼淚後將手插進口袋，四下張望的同時喃喃說道：「但現在太遲了。」

「什麼事？」精靈問道。

「沒什麼。」施顧己說：「沒什麼。昨天晚上有一個男孩在我的門口唱聖誕頌歌。我想我應該給他點什麼的，如此而已。」

精靈親切一笑，揮揮手說道：「我們看看另一個聖誕吧！」

它這麼一說，昔日的施顧己便長大了些，房間也變得更暗、更髒。鑲板減少了，窗戶裂了縫，天花板上的灰泥片片掉落，板條也裸露在外，這番景象是怎麼變出來的，施顧己也和你們一樣莫明其妙。他只知道景象十分真切，事情的確是這樣沒有錯，他又是一個人，其他孩子早就歡歡喜喜回家過節了。

這回他不是在看書，而是沮喪地踱來踱去。施顧己看著精靈，一面悲哀地搖頭，一面焦慮地往門口張望。

門開了，一個比男孩年紀小得多的小女孩衝了進來，雙臂環抱住他的頸子，不停地親他，還稱呼他作「親愛的，親愛的哥哥」。

「親愛的哥哥，我來帶你回家！」小女孩拍著小手說，還笑彎了腰：「帶你回家，回家，回家！」

「回家，小芬？」男孩應道。

「對！」小女孩歡天喜地地說：「回家，再也不離開了。永遠、永遠住在家裡。爸爸比以前和藹多了，家就像天堂一樣！有一個美麗的夜晚，我正要上床的時候，他跟我說話的口氣好輕好柔，所以我也就不害怕又問他一次你可不可以回家。他說可以，你應該回家的，然後就讓我搭車來找你了。你要變成大人了！」小女孩張大了眼睛說：「永遠也不用再回這裡來。不過，整個聖誕節我們還是可以一起過，過全世界最快樂的日子。」

「妳真是長大了，小芬！」男孩喊道。

她拍著手笑，還想摸摸他的頭，但因太矮搆不著，便又笑著踮起腳尖去抱他。然後，她孩子氣地拉著哥哥急急往門口走，而他也正中下懷地跟著她出去。

門廳裡有個可怕的聲音喊道：「來，把施顧己同學的箱子拿下來！」校長親自來到門廳，一個勁地瞪著施顧己看，故意表示親切熱絡，還跟他握手，嚇得他心裡七上八下的。接著校長領著這對兄妹走進一間冷冰冰的會客室，這裡簡直就是全世界最溼冷的老舊地窖，就連掛在牆上的地圖和擺在窗台上的天象儀和地球儀，也都罩上一層冷霜。他拿出一瓶淡得出奇的葡萄酒和一塊重得出奇的蛋糕，並將這些美食點心分給兩個小孩吃，同時還派一位瘦巴巴的僕人出去問問車夫，想不想喝點什麼；車夫謝過校長的美意，並回說如果喝的和上次一樣，那還是不用了。此時施顧己同學的行李箱已經綁上馬車車頂，兩個孩子欣然向校長道別後，爬上馬車，高高興興地駛下庭園的彎道，車輪飛馳而過，濺起覆蓋在常綠灌木深色樹葉上的霜雪，像一波波的白浪。

「她總是那麼嬌弱，弱不禁風的。」精靈說：「但她有顆寬容的心！」

「的確，」施顧己說：「精靈，你說得沒錯，這點我不否認，否則老天也不饒我！」

「她結婚以後才去世，」精靈說：「好像還有小孩了。」

「有一個小孩。」施顧己回答道。

「對，」精靈說：「你的外甥！」

施顧己內心顯得不安，只簡單地回了一句：「是的。」

雖然他們才剛剛離開學校，卻馬上就來到了繁忙的市區街道，熙來攘往的人影幢幢，爭先恐後的二輪與四輪馬車車影幢幢，儼然一副城市該有的喧囂擾攘。從店面的裝飾一眼就能看出，又是聖誕節到了，但此時已經入夜，街上都亮起了燈。

精靈在一間商號的門口站定，問施顧己認不認得。

「認得！」施顧己說：「我不就是在這裡當學徒的嗎？」

他們走了進去。有一位戴著威爾斯假髮的老先生坐在一張很高很高的桌子後面，他要是再高個兩吋，頭都要頂到天花板了。施顧己一看到他，便興奮地嚷著……

「是老費茲維呢！老天保佑。費茲維又活過來了！」

老費茲維將筆擱下，抬頭看看時鐘，時針指著七點。他搓搓手，整整他寬大的背心，開懷大笑，整個人從頭——這是他仁慈的泉源——到腳都暢快不已，然後用他輕鬆圓潤、響亮飽滿的聲音愉快地喊道……

「喂，來呀！艾布內茲！迪克！」

施顧已從前的自己當時已經是個小夥子，只見他和另一名學徒踩著輕快的腳步走進來。

「果然是迪克·威肯斯！」施顧已對精靈說：「呵，真的是他。他跟我感情非常好呀，這個迪克。可憐的迪克！天哪，天哪！」

「來呀，孩子們！」費茲維說：「今晚不用做事了。聖誕夜呀，迪克。過聖誕了，艾布內茲！上板了吧。」老費茲用力拍了一下手喊道：「馬上行動！」

你一定不相信那兩個小夥子動作有多快！他們扛起窗板衝到街上……

一、二、三……放到定位……四、五、六……上門釘牢……七、八、九……你都還沒來得及數到十二，他們就氣喘如牛地跑回來了。

「來吧！」老費茲維喊道，一面從高高的桌上跳下來，行動十分敏捷：「孩子們，東西清乾淨，把這裡全空出來！來吧，迪克！快，艾布內茲！」

清乾淨！有老費茲維盯著，每樣東西都清得乾乾淨淨，也不可能清不乾淨。才一轉眼就全做好了。所有可移動的東西都速速撤走，彷彿從此再也不能出現在公開場合；地板掃了又洗，燈芯修剪了，火爐裡的煤炭塊也堆得高高的，商號一下子變成冬夜裡人人期盼得見的一個又暖和又舒適、又乾燥又明亮的舞廳。

一個小提琴手來了，他帶著樂譜站上高高的桌面，把那兒當成演奏席，調音的時候像是有五十個肚子痛的病患發出哀號。費茲維太太來了，豐腴的臉上笑盈盈的。三位費茲維小姐來了，光彩照人、美麗動人。六名為她們心碎的追求者來了。所有的年輕男女僱員都來了。女僕和她的表兄——一位麵包師傅——來了。女廚子和她哥哥的好友——一個送牛奶的工人——來了。對街的男孩也來了，聽說在主人家裡經常挨餓，只見他在一個女孩身後躲躲藏藏，女孩則是隔壁第二家的，老被女主人揪耳朵。他們一個接著一個，全進來了；有人害羞，有人大膽，有人優雅，有人怪異，有人迫不及待，有人拖拖拉拉；無論如何，總而言之，他們全都來了。

二十對一下子全跳起舞來，拉著手跳半圈再跳回起點，跳到中央又往回跳，大夥轉呀轉呀，興高采烈地交換舞伴。原本領頭的一對老是跳錯位置，後來領頭的一到定位也不等人便自顧自地跳起來，最後每一對都成了領頭的，後面卻一個人也沒有。到了這個地步，老費維茲便會拍手讓大家停下來，並大喊：「跳得好！」而小提琴手便會趁這個時候將熱烘烘的臉埋進一大罐黑啤酒當中，這酒正是專門準備來讓他浸臉用的。但當他一抬頭也不休息，雖然還沒有人跳舞，他卻立刻又演奏起來，好像前一個提琴手已經筋疲力盡，被人用門板抬回家去，如今換上一個全新的樂手，誓言要將前一個樂師徹底擊敗，不成功便成仁。

大夥又跳了幾支舞，玩了幾個遊戲，再跳幾支舞，接著便享用餐點，有蛋糕、尼格斯酒、一大塊烤肉冷盤、一大塊白煮肉冷盤、碎肉餡餅，還有大量的啤酒。不過，在烤肉與白煮肉上來之後，當小提琴手（相信我，他可是個機靈的傢伙！什麼時候該奏什麼曲子，這種人心知肚明，無須你我多言！）開始拉起〈羅傑柯弗利老爺〉這支舞曲，才算進入了當晚的重頭戲。

於是老費維茲起身與妻子共舞。他們自然是領頭的一對，任務可一點也不輕鬆：二十三、四對的舞伴跟在後頭，這些人全都不容小覷，他們是來跳舞，可不是來散步的。

但是即使人數多上兩倍，不，應該說是四倍，老費維茲仍然應付得來，費維茲太太也一樣。她呢，在各方面都是費維茲的最佳拍檔。假如這麼稱讚還不夠，倒請說說還有什麼更高的讚譽，我馬上改口。費維茲的雙腿彷彿射出了光線，像兩彎月亮似的照亮了每一個舞步；無論什麼時候，你都猜不出他下一步會怎麼跳。當老費維茲和太太跳完所有的舞步：前進、後退，牽舞伴的手、鞠躬、屈膝、迴旋、再一個穿針引線，回原位之後，費維茲還躍起身來，雙腿在空中交互擊打，動作快得像眨眼似的，接著雙腳一落地，晃也沒晃一下。

十一的鐘聲響起，這個家庭舞會便散會了。費維茲夫婦在大門兩側各就定位，和每個離去的人握手，並祝他們聖誕快樂。當所有的人都離開，只剩

下兩名學徒時，他們也同樣向學徒握手祝賀。於是愉快的聲音漸漸遠去，小

夥計也上了床，床就在店面後間的一個櫃台底下。

這一大段時間裡，施顧己活像一個神志不清的人，他的心神與靈魂都融

進了那個畫面，和從前的自己在一起。他證實了一切，想起了一切，享受著

一切，並感受到一種奇怪無比的興奮情緒。一直到從前的他和迪克那兩張明亮

的臉龐轉了過去，他才想起精靈，也才意識到它正盯著自己看，而它頭上那

束光照得更加耀眼了。

「小事一椿，」精靈說：「就讓這些愚蠢的傢伙感激涕零了。」

「小事！」施顧己重覆著它的話。

精靈示意他聽聽兩個學徒的談話，他二人正互相傾吐心聲，讚美著費維

茲。他聽完後，精靈說：

「難道不是嗎？他也只不過花了你們人世間的幾個銅板，大概三四英鎊

吧，就值得這麼稱讚了？」

「話不能這麼說。」施顧己聽了這番話不覺激動起來，說話的口氣也不知

不覺變成從前的他，而不是後來的他⋯「話不能這麼說，精靈。他有能力決定

讓我們快樂或不快樂，讓我們的工作輕鬆或沉重，是樂趣或是苦役。就算他以言語與表情，以一些微不足道的小事來傳達這份能力，那又如何？他所帶來的快樂卻是一筆大大的財富。」

他感覺到精靈看了自己一眼，便立即住口。

「怎麼了？」精靈問道。

「沒什麼。」施顧己說。

「我想一定有事？」精靈很堅持。

「沒有。」施顧己說：「沒有。我只是覺得剛才應該跟我的夥計說一兩句話！如此而已。」

施顧己說著這個希望的同時，從前的他也關了燈，於是他和精靈再次肩並肩地站到戶外來了。

「我的時間越來越少了，」精靈說：「快點！」

這句話不是對施顧己或是任何他看得見的人說的，但馬上便產生了效應。因為施顧己又見到了自己，這回他年紀又大了些，正值壯年時期，他的臉上還沒有出現後來幾年的那些嚴酷、僵硬的線條，不過已經開始顯現計較與貪婪的神色。骨碌碌轉動的眼睛裡有一種貪慾與急切，由此可見已在他心中扎根的那份狂熱，也由此可知扎了根的樹長大後樹影該會朝哪兒落。

他並非一個人，他身旁坐著一位穿著喪服、年輕又漂亮的女子…她的眼中噙著淚水，映著過去的聖誕精靈所射出的光芒閃閃發亮。

「無所謂，」她輕輕地說：「對你來說，一點也無所謂。你已經有另外一個偶像來取代我了。我本來希望能在未來的日子裡帶給你歡樂與慰藉，但假如它能做到，我也就沒有理由悲傷了。」

「有什麼偶像取代了妳？」施顧己反問。

「一個黃金偶像 5。」

「這個世界可真是太公平了哦！」他說：「對貧窮的人它殘酷而不假辭色，對於追求財富的人它卻又如此嚴厲地指責！」

「你太在乎世人的眼光了。」她輕聲回答道：「你原本有許多希望，後來卻變得只求不受勢利的世人批判。我親眼見到你的宏圖大志一個一個地破滅，最後只剩一樣讓你情有獨鍾，那就是利益。我說得對不對？」

「那又怎麼樣？」他反駁道：「就算我現在變得聰明得多，那又怎麼樣？

「我對妳可沒變。」

她搖搖頭。

「我變了？」

「我們的誓約已經過時了。當時我們都很窮，也不怨天尤人，只期待有一天能憑藉著我們的勤奮改善經濟情況。但你的確是變了，你已經不是當初立誓時候的你了。」

「我當時年紀還小。」他不耐地說。

「你也感覺到自己和從前不一樣。」她答道：「但我沒變。當初我們心意相連時所感覺到的幸福，如今卻因為貌合神離而成了痛苦的泉源。我有多常想到這點，想得心有多痛，也就不必說了。重要的是我想到過，所以現在你可以解脫了。」

「我曾經想過要解脫嗎？」

「口頭上沒有，從來沒有。」

「那我是怎麼表達的呢？」

「從你性格的變化，從你觀點的改變，從你不同的生活環境，從你不同的人生目標，還有那些曾經使你重視我的愛情的一切。如果我們之間沒有這個約定，」女孩望著他，神色和緩但眼神堅定：「你告訴我，你現在還會約我出來，試圖贏得我的心嗎？不，不會的！」

他似乎不由自主便默認了這個假設。但他還是勉強說了一句：「那是妳自己想的。」

「可能的話，我也很想有別的想法。」她回答說：「老天可以作證！要我接受這樣一個事實，那它必定是非常強而有力。但假如今天、明天、昨天的你可以自由選擇，叫我如何相信你──這個即使說著悄悄話，也是一切以利益為前提的你──會選擇一個沒有嫁妝的女孩？或者你因為一時衝動而選擇了她，我又怎麼會不知道你將來一定會懊惱、會後悔？我知道，所以我讓你解脫。我誠心誠意，因為我曾經愛過從前的那個你。」

他正打算開口，但她一掉頭又接著說：

「也許吧，回想起過去，我想你應該會覺得難過。非常、非常短暫的時間過後，你便會欣然屏除這段回憶，就好像慶幸自己及時從一個無利可圖的夢中醒來一樣。但願在你選擇的生活裡，你能活得快樂！」

她離開了他，他們分手了。

「精靈！」施顧己說：「別讓我再看下去了！帶我回家吧。為什麼你要這麼折磨我？」

「再看一場幻影吧！」幽靈大喊。

「不了！」施顧己嚷著：「不了。我不想看了，別讓我再看下去！」

但是鐵石心腸的幽靈用雙手緊緊抱住他，逼著他看接下來發生的事。

他們又到了另一個場景與地點：一個不太大也不太華麗的房間，不過相當舒適。冬天的爐火旁坐著一位美麗的年輕女子，像極了剛才那位，施顧己原以為是同一人，直到他看見了坐在女子對面的「她」，才知道美麗如昔的她已嫁為人婦，這年輕女子是她的女兒。房裡的噪音喧天，因為裡頭的孩子多得讓施顧己紛亂的心怎麼也數不清；這些小孩可不像名詩人詩中所寫的「四十頭牛全都一個樣」[6]，反倒是每個人都像有四十個化身。結果自然是吵翻了天，但似乎並無人在意，母女倆倒反而笑得開懷，樂在其中。不久，女兒也加入了混戰，卻遭到這群小土匪猛烈無情的攻擊。要是能加入他們，我還有什麼捨不得付出的呢！不過我絕對不會如此魯莽，不，決不！即使給我全世界的財富，我也不會拉扯那髮辮讓它散落，而那隻可愛的小鞋，我也不會硬生生將它剝下，我可以對天發誓！我死也不會這麼做。至於那些野蠻的小傢伙開玩笑說要量她的腰身，這事我也不可能去做，因為我擔心老天為了懲罰我，會讓我的胳臂彎成腰身的弧形，再也伸不直。然而坦白說，我真希望能碰碰她的嘴唇，能問她一個問題，好讓她輕啟朱唇，能凝視她低垂的睫毛卻不使她臉紅，能撥弄她波浪形的秀髮，因為那每一吋髮絲都將是一份無價的紀念⋯⋯總之我承認，我希望自己能享受到小孩放肆的特權，即使一丁點也好，但又已經成熟到足以認清這份特權的價值。

此時忽然傳來一陣敲門聲，那群臉上紅撲撲、嬉鬧不止的孩子，立刻簇擁著滿臉笑意，衣裳凌亂的女孩衝上前去，剛好及時將回家的父親迎進門來，另外還跟著一個人提著大包小包的聖誕玩具與禮物。接著便是一陣叫囂與拉扯，提著禮物的人遭到襲擊也無力抵抗！只見他們拿椅子墊高，爬到他身上，一頭鑽進他的袋子，搶奪用包裝紙包著的禮物，緊緊拉住他的領帶，抱住他的脖子，猛捶他的背，還直踢他的腳，簡直興奮地昏了頭！每個包裹一打開，總會引來驚嘆與歡呼聲連連！有人發出驚呼，因為小嬰兒正要把洋娃娃的平底鍋塞進嘴巴，而且很可能已經吞下一隻黏在木盤上的紙火雞！後來發現只是虛驚一場，大夥才大大鬆了口氣！他們的歡樂、感恩與狂喜，全都無法形容。只能說漸漸地孩子們帶著他們興奮的情緒離開了客廳，一步一階地爬到樓頂，然後上了床，一切才歸於平靜。

此時施顧己看得更加專注了，因為男主人走到火爐邊，面對著妻子坐下來，女兒則輕輕地依偎在他身旁。施顧己一想到如此優雅而充滿希望的女孩，原可能是自己的女兒，原本可能為他人生的寒冬注入春意，他的視線不禁越來越模糊了。

「貝兒，」丈夫微笑著轉向妻子說道：「今天下午，我看到你一位老朋友。」

「誰呀？」

「猜猜看！」

「我怎麼猜得到？哎呀，該不會是……」她也和丈夫一樣笑著，緊接著又說：「施顧己先生。」

「正是施顧己先生。」我從他辦公室的窗前經過，當時窗子沒關，裡頭點了一根蠟燭，忍不住就往裡看了一下。聽說他的合夥人快要嚥氣了，他一個人坐在那兒，我想他一定很孤單。」

「精靈！」施顧己以嘶啞的聲音說：「帶我離開這個地方。」

「我說過這些都是過去事物的幻影。」幽靈說：「事實就是如此，怪不得我！」

「帶我走！」施顧己大叫：「我受不了了！」

他轉向幽靈，見它正盯著自己看，奇怪的是剛才看見的所有臉孔竟都有一小部分出現在它臉上，他立刻衝上去扭住了它。

「你走！帶我回去！別再來騷擾我了！」

在一陣打鬥之中──如果這也能稱之為打鬥的話，因為幽靈方面並無明顯的反抗動作，對於對手所使出的任何力道也無動於衷──施顧己發現幽靈的光芒射得又高又亮；他隱約覺得它對自己的影響與這道光有關，於是抓起滅光帽，一個反手便將帽子往它頭上壓。

精靈應勢而倒，整頂滅光帽將它團團蓋住，但儘管施顧己死命地往下壓，卻仍掩蓋不住光芒，只見一絲絲光線從帽子底下源源不斷地滲出，溢滿了地面。

他感覺自己精疲力盡，濃濃的睡意襲將上來，接著便發現已經回到自己的臥室。他最後又用力壓了帽子一下才鬆手，然後搖搖晃晃走到床邊，一倒下便睡得不省人事。

註：

1.引自《天方夜譚》（一千零一夜）中的〈阿里巴巴和四十大盜的故事〉；阿里巴巴與妻子過著清貧的生活，住在一間破屋內，每天趕著三匹毛驢到山林中砍柴，再將木柴馱到市集變賣。

2. 在中世紀傳說中，瓦倫泰（Valentine）和奧森（Orso）是一對雙胞胎兄弟，與父親流浪者貝利森特在森林裡走失；瓦倫泰長大後成為一位彬彬有禮的青年，奧丁則被母熊撫養長大，成為中世紀的妖怪野人。

3. 狄更斯童年時，最喜愛的書籍之一是《天方夜譚》（一千零一夜），在書信及文章中經常提起這本書。

4. 出自《魯賓遜漂流記》（*Robinson Crusoe*, 1719）小說中的人物和情節。一次，魯賓遜展開他冒險的水手生涯時，卻遇上暴風雨，獨自一人漂流到荒島。他和狗、貓、一隻鸚鵡一起生活，並在荒島上遇見第一個人類「星期五」。

5. 黃金偶像──出自《出埃及記》中的典故：當摩西登上西乃山，聽取神所諭示的十誡時，以色列人卻用金子鑄造一隻牛犢，作為神像崇拜。

6. 出自英國浪漫派詩人威廉・華茲華斯（William Worsworth, 1770—1850）的詩作〈三月〉（*Written in March*, 1802）組詩中的一首。

The cock is crowing,
The stream is flowing,
The all birds twitter,
The lake doth glitter

The green field sleeps in the sun :
The oldest and youngest
Are at work with the strongest :
The cattle are grazing,
Their heads never raising :
There are forty feeding like one.

三個精靈中的第二個

施顧己在一聲震天價響的鼾聲中醒來，從床上坐起集中精神之後，用不著他人提醒便知道一點的鐘聲又快響了。他覺得自己的意識恢復得正是時候，專就為了和雅各‧馬利所安排來的第二位使者會談。可是當他一想到這個新來的幽靈不知道會拉起哪一邊的床帷時，突然覺得自己全身發冷很不舒服，於是他便親自動手將兩邊的帷幔都拉開，然後重新躺下，提高警覺地監視著床四周的動靜。因為他希望在精靈出現的時候能勇敢以對，而不想因為沒有做好心理準備而手足無措、緊張兮兮。

那些性格豪放不拘的男士們，經常誇口自己什麼大風大浪都見過，任何局面都能應付自如，好像個個有通天本領，不管擲錢的遊戲或殺人的勾當，都難不倒他們；在擲錢與殺人這兩個極端之間自然是範圍廣泛、包羅萬象。我不敢這麼大膽地為施顧己打包票，不過我可以請各位相信，他確實已經準備好目睹千奇百怪的形貌，不管出現的是嬰兒還是犀牛，他都不會太訝異。

然而，雖然幾乎已經做好一切的準備，可是他壓根也沒想到會毫無動靜，因此當一點的鐘聲響後，卻沒有幽靈出現，他竟全身抖個不停。五分鐘、十分鐘、十五分鐘過去了，還是一點動靜也沒有。這段時間裡他一直躺在床上，床的四周圍繞著一片火紅的光，那是鐘敲響一點整的時候灑進來的。雖然只是一片光線，卻比十數個鬼魂還要令人心驚，因為他根本猜不出它代表著什麼，或預示了什麼。有幾回他甚至擔心：說不定自己當時已經成為一個有趣的自燃案例，卻還懵然不知。不過最後他忽然想到了——這其實是你我一開始就想到的；因為向來都是旁觀者才知道該怎麼做，並能夠確實付諸行動——我剛剛說了，最後他終於想到這道幽靈般光線的神祕來源可能就在隔壁房間，因為他循線望去，發現光線似乎就是從那兒射出來的。他腦子裡不斷轉著這個念頭，於是輕輕地下了床，趿著拖鞋便往門邊走去。

施顧己的手才一摸到門鎖，就聽到一個奇怪的聲音叫著他的名字，請他進去。他也就進去了。

那是他自己的房間，絕對錯不了。可是這會兒卻完全走了樣。牆壁上和天花板上全都垂掛著綠葉，像極了一個小樹林，到處還有晶瑩剔透的漿果閃閃發亮。光線從冬青、槲寄生與常春藤清新的葉子[1]上反射回來，四下彷彿擺滿了一面面的小鏡子。還有那麼一股熊熊火焰，呼嘯著衝上煙囪，這個向來陰冷蕭條的壁爐可從來沒有經歷過這樣的待遇，不管是在施顧己的時代、在馬利的時代，或是在那許許多多過往的冬日都沒有經歷過。地板上的食物一樣又一樣堆得高高的像個王座，其中有火雞、鵝、野味、雞鴨、肉凍、大大的肉塊、乳豬、成串的香腸、碎肉餅、一桶一桶的鮮蠔、燙手的栗子、紅通通的蘋果、多汁的柳橙、甜美的梨子、巨大的主顯節蛋糕[2]和熱騰騰的潘趣酒，那香甜的蒸汽瀰漫得整個房間霧濛濛的。在這高高的寶座上坐著一個神情悠閒愉快的巨人，好一幅壯觀的畫面⋯它擎著一把灼灼的火炬，形狀倒挺像「豐饒的角」，當施顧己在門邊窺探時，巨人便將火炬高高舉起，讓火光照在施顧己身上。

「進來吧！」幽靈喊道：「進來！多認識認識我，老兄！」

施顧己怯怯地走進去，在精靈面前低垂著頭。他已經不是原來那個頑固的施顧己，雖然精靈的眼睛明亮而和善，他卻不想接觸它的目光。

「我是現在的聖誕精靈，」幽靈說：「抬頭看著我！」

於是施顧己便畢恭畢敬地抬起頭來。這精靈身上只穿著一件有白色皮毛滾邊、樣式簡單的深綠色袍子，或者說是斗篷。這件長衣鬆鬆垮垮地披在它身上，一大片胸脯裸露在外，好像不屑於用任何方式加以掩護或遮蓋似的。袍子下襬層層疊疊的褶子下方，也露出一雙赤腳，而它頭上則只戴了一頂冬青花冠，花冠上還隨意裝飾著幾根閃亮的小冰柱。它披散著長長的深褐色捲髮：就跟它和顏悅色的臉龐、它閃閃發亮的眼睛、它敞開的手掌、它愉快的聲音、它無拘無束的態度與它歡喜的神情一樣隨性。它腰間配帶著一柄古老的劍鞘，但裡頭沒有劍，鞘殼則已銹跡斑斑。

「你從來沒見過像我這樣的吧！」精靈大聲說道。

「從來沒有。」施顧己回答。

「從來沒有接觸過我那些年紀較輕的家人？我指的是在這幾年才出生的哥哥們（因為我還非常年輕）。」幽靈又問。

「我想應該沒有。」施顧己說：「恐怕是沒有的。你有很多兄弟嗎，精靈？」

「有一千八百多個。」幽靈說。

「這可是一大家子要養啊！」施顧己嘀咕著。

這時現在的聖誕精靈站起身來。

「精靈，」施顧己順從地說：「你想帶我到哪裡去都行。昨天晚上我是被強迫著去的，我也得了個教訓，所以現在學乖了。今晚，假如你有任何指教，我一定悉心受教。」

「摸著我的袍子！」

施顧己照著它的話做，而且抓得牢牢的。

冬青、檞寄生、紅漿果、常春藤、火雞、鵝、野味、雞鴨、肉凍、肉塊、豬隻、香腸、生蠔、肉餅、布丁、水果和酒，一轉眼全都不見了。還有房間、火爐、紅光、夜晚也都消失了，他們就站在聖誕節早晨的市區街道上。

由於氣候酷寒，家家戶戶都忙著刮去門前人行道上和屋頂上的雪，發出一種粗糙，但輕快又不怎麼難聽的樂音。一旁的小男孩看著屋頂積雪轟的一聲砸落在底下的路面，飛散成一陣陣小型的人造暴風雪，個個都樂歪了。

屋子的正面看起來真夠黑的，窗框更黑，和屋頂上那一大片平滑的白雪，以及地面上較髒的雪形成強烈對比。笨重的貨車與馬車駛過時就像犁田一樣，在地面最上層的積雪上留下一道又一道深深的轍痕，這些轍痕在大街的路口相互交疊千百次，形成了錯綜複雜的渠道，而渠道淹沒在摻雜著冰水的黃色泥漿之下，已然辨識不出方向。天陰陰的，所有的大街小巷都瀰漫著一層灰霧³，霧氣中半是水半是冰，較重的粒子像一顆顆的小碳粒傾盆而落，倒像是全英國的煙囪都不約而同地起了火，劈哩啪啦地燒得興致正高。無論是天候或市街都沒有特別歡樂的氣氛，然而四下裡卻洋溢著一種喜氣，就算是再晴朗的夏日、再豔麗的夏陽，恐怕也很難散播出這樣的歡樂。

因為在屋頂上鏟雪的人個個心情愉快、歡天喜地，站在護欄邊互相叫喚，偶爾開個玩笑互丟雪球——這些飛彈遠比一些口頭的玩笑更無惡意——丟準了便開懷大笑，丟得不準也同樣快活。賣雞鴨的店家門還半開著，水果店卻是聲勢浩大、琳琅滿目。

裝著栗子的圓滾滾的大簍子，就像幾個樂天的老先生挺著個大肚子，懶懶地靠在門邊，而大得幾乎動彈不得的肚子則都凸到街上來了。一個個表皮棕褐、紅潤、腰圍粗大的西班牙洋蔥，油油亮亮的活像西班牙的修道士，它們輕佻頑皮地朝著過路的女孩眨眼，偶爾卻又靦腆地覷一覷高掛在頂上的槲寄生。還有梨子和蘋果高高疊起，成了一座又一座的大金字塔；好心的店家還將串串葡萄懸在醒目的掛鉤上，免費供過往行人觀賞垂涎；還有一堆堆長滿絨毛的褐色榛果，那香味不由得令人想起樹林間的古老步道，以及緩緩涉過深及足踝的枯葉的樂趣；還有矮矮胖胖的諾福克紅蘋果，那暗紅色澤將柳橙與檸檬襯托得更為鮮黃，只見蘋果挺著密實多汁的身軀，急切地懇請並哀求著路人把它們裝進牛皮紙袋裡帶回家，飯後享用。

形形色色的水果之間還擺了一只魚缸，裡頭金色、銀色的魚雖然冷血又麻木，卻似乎也知道外頭有那麼一點不同，便張著嘴，帶著一種溫吞、不甚熱衷的興奮，在它們的小世界裡游來游去。

雜貨店！雜貨店哪！差不多就要關了，大概只剩下一兩面窗板還沒裝上；不過從那些細縫裡瞥見的景象可有多美！倒不是因為櫃台上的秤盤發出美妙的聲響，或是麻繩從捲軸上快速切斷的聲音，或是金屬罐變戲法似的上上下下忙得匡噹作響，或是茶葉混合著咖啡的香氣撲鼻，又或是許許多多的葡萄乾樣樣罕見，杏仁潔白無瑕，肉桂又長又直，其他的香料美味可口，還有糖漬水果裹著一層厚厚的、不均勻的糖衣，讓再怎麼不受誘惑的人看了也不禁要為之暈眩，甚至胃絞痛。

也不是因為無花果個個溫潤而飽滿，或是裝在五顏六色的盒子裡的法國酸李發出微紅微紅的色澤，又或是店裡所有的東西都既可口又裝點著聖誕節的喜氣。而是因為顧客們太過於匆匆忙忙，迫不及待想要體驗這個日子所應有的歡樂，因此一到門口便撞個滿懷，購物籃也被用力地擠來擠去都壓扁了，還把買了的東西忘在櫃台上，之後又趕緊跑回來拿，儘管類似的差錯難以計數，卻還是人人保持著無比的好心情。而雜貨店主人和夥計對人更是熱忱而親切，別在他們圍裙背後那顆閃亮的金屬彷彿就是他們自己的心，暴露在外好讓大夥都看得見，就算聖誕寒鴉想要啄一啄也歡迎。

但是不久尖塔的鐘聲便呼喚著老百姓前往教堂與禮拜堂，於是大家穿上了最體面的衣服，帶著最愉快的面容，魚貫似的穿過街道而來。這個時候，從許多街道巷弄與無名的街口轉角處，冒出了成群成群的人捧著晚餐朝麵包店走去。見到這些準備歡宴的窮人似乎讓精靈興味盎然，它和施顧己並肩站在一間麵包店門口，一有人捧著晚餐走過去，4它便掀開蓋子，然後用火炬在他們的晚餐上頭撒下一點香灰。那可不是一把普通的火炬，因為有一兩次捧著晚餐的人彼此推擠，差點發生口角，只見它拿起火炬往他們頭上灑了幾滴水，他們立刻又恢復了好脾氣。他們說了，在聖誕節吵架實在太過分。可不是嘛！老天有眼，可不是這樣嘛！

鐘聲漸漸停息了，麵包店也關了門，不過令人欣慰的是晚餐似乎已經都進了烤爐，因為每個麵包店爐子上的雪都融解成一大片水跡，甚至人行道上都冒起煙來，彷彿連磚石也正忙著煮食。

「你火炬裡撒出來的東西有特別的味道嗎？」施顧己說。

「有。有我獨特的風味。」

「對這一天的任何一種晚餐都能產生效應嗎？」施顧己問道。

「對任何一種善心的施予都有效。越貧乏的越有效。」

「為什麼越貧乏的越有效？」施顧己問。

「因為這樣的晚餐更需要。」

「精靈，」施顧己想了一會，說道：「我覺得很吃驚，因為在我們的四周有許多不同的世界，而生活在這些世界裡的所有個體之中，只有你想約束這些窮人，使他們無法享受純真的喜悅。」

「我！」精靈大叫。

「你每七天便要剝奪他們用餐的機會，而這一天卻通常是他們唯一可以用餐的日子，不是這樣嗎？」

「我！」精靈大叫。

「你不是企圖讓這些店在安息日都關門嗎？」施顧己說：「那麼結果是一樣的。」

「我企圖！」精靈大叫。

「如果我說錯了，請你原諒。因為大家都是以你，或至少是以你們家人的名義才這麼做的。」施顧己說。

「在你們這個地球上，」精靈反駁道：「有些人自稱認識我們，便打著我們的名號從事他們自己狂熱、驕傲、惡毒、仇恨、忌妒、偏執與自私的行為。這些人對我們以及我們所有的親人而言，就像從來不曾存在過的陌生人一樣。記住這一點，他們要為自己的行為負責，不要怪我們。」

施顧己答應了之後，他們又像先前一般，隱身進入郊區。幽靈有一點很了不起（這是施顧己在麵包店發現的），儘管它身形龐大，卻還是可以輕易地在任何地方安身。就算站在低矮的屋簷下，它也依然能夠保持幽靈的優雅氣度，就像身處於宏偉挑高的大廳一樣。

或許善心的精靈樂於展現自己這份神力，也或許是因為它善良、慷慨、熱心的本質以及對窮人的憐憫，它直接就找上了施顧己的夥計，身邊還帶著緊抓住它的袍子的施顧己。精靈微笑地在門口站定，拿起火炬撒下它對鮑伯‧克拉契一家人的祝福。想想看！鮑伯一個禮拜只賺十五先令，每個禮拜六他也只能在口袋裡放進這十五個銅板，而現在的聖誕精靈竟然降福在他這間四房的住家！

此時克拉契太太——也就是鮑伯的妻子——站起身來，她穿著自己最美的衣服，卻只是翻身改製過兩次的一件舊衣，不過倒是紮了許多緞帶，這些緞帶很便宜，花幾個便士就能增添美觀。她鋪上桌布準備用餐，二女兒白琳達在一旁幫忙，身上的緞帶也和母親的一樣多；至於長子彼得‧克拉契正拿起叉子朝那一鍋的馬鈴薯戳，嘴裡咬著巨大的襯衫衣領（這本是鮑伯的私產，他趁著這個特殊的日子，贈給了兒子兼繼承人），他對自己如此盛裝打扮興奮莫名，並且迫不及待想到時髦人士出沒的公園裡去秀一秀。這時候，克拉契家兩個較小的孩子，一男一女，衝了進來，叫喊著說他們在麵包店外面就聞到鵝肉的香味，而且馬上就知道是自己家的。兩個小孩一心幻想著洋蘇草與洋蔥的香氣，高興得在桌邊跳起舞來，還把彼得．克拉契捧上了天，而彼得（雖然被衣領勒得快要窒息，卻還是若無其事地）吹著爐火，直到一整鍋懶洋洋的馬鈴薯終於沸騰，撲撲地敲打鍋蓋，好像在求人趕緊將它們拿出來剝皮。

「你那寶貝父親是怎麼回事？」克拉契太太說：「還有你弟弟小提姆，還有瑪莎，去年聖誕節她可沒遲到半個小時呢！」

「媽，瑪莎來了！」女兒跑進來說。

「媽，瑪莎來了！」兩個小傢伙喊道：「萬歲！瑪莎！有好大一隻鵝哦！」

「老天，妳可真慢哪，親愛的！」克拉契太太不斷親她，一面替她取下披肩與帽子，親熱得不得了。

「昨天晚上有好多工作要結束，」女孩回道：「今天早上還得清理乾淨呀，媽媽！」

「好啦，人回來了就好。」克拉契太太說：「到火爐邊坐著去吧，親愛的，去烤烤火！」

「不要，不要！」兩個小傢伙跑來跑去地嚷著：「爸爸來了，躲起來，瑪莎，躲起來！」

於是瑪莎便躲了起來，只見他們的父親小鮑伯走進來，胸前垂著一條至少三呎長的圍巾（流蘇還不算在內），毛絨已經磨光的衣服還特意縫補、刷平，以便像個過節的樣子，肩上則扛著小提姆。可憐的小提姆，他提著一根小拐杖，兩隻腳還用金屬架撐著！

「咦，我們的瑪莎呢？」鮑伯·克拉契四下看了看，嚷著說。

「沒回來。」克拉契太太說。

「沒回來！」鮑伯忽然整個人洩了氣似的，因為他剛才讓小提姆跨坐在肩頭，一路從教堂狂奔回來。「聖誕節都不回來！」

瑪莎不想見他失望，雖然只是開開玩笑，因此她不再等便從壁櫥的門後跑出來，衝進他的懷中，而兩個小傢伙則推擁著小提姆進洗衣房去，好讓他聽聽布丁在大水鍋裡唱歌。

「小提姆乖不乖啊？」當鮑伯開心地摟著女兒，克拉契太太挪揄了他一陣之後問道。

「乖得像小綿羊，」鮑伯說：「甚至更乖呢。不知怎地他老是一個人坐在旁邊，想一些稀奇古怪的事情。回家的路上他對我說，他希望能上教堂讓大家看看，因為他雙腳殘廢，看到他大夥就會在聖誕節這天想起耶穌讓跛腳乞丐可以走路、盲人可以重見天日，這應該是件令人高興的事。」

鮑伯說這些話的時候聲音有些顫抖，當他說到小提姆越來越堅強、越強壯時，聲音更是抖得厲害。

他們聽見他那支活動小拐杖敲在地板上的聲音，還沒接著說下去，就看到小提姆在哥哥、姊姊的護送下走向火爐邊的小板凳。這個時候鮑伯捲起袖子——可憐的傢伙，那袖口難道還可能弄得更髒、更寒傖嗎？——把雜七雜八的一些熱食倒進鉢裡，再加入杜松子酒和檸檬，攪拌又攪拌之後放到壁爐的火上以文火加熱。長子彼得和那兩個跑來跑去的弟妹去端鵝肉，不久便見他們一行浩浩蕩蕩地回來了。

他們進門所引起的一陣騷動，還真讓人以為鵝是「世上最稀有的鳥類」，彷彿是一隻罕見的珍禽異獸，就連黑天鵝也自歎弗如；事實上，在這屋裡的情形也差不多就是這樣。克拉契太太將事先便已備妥在一只長柄燉鍋裡的肉汁加熱，長子彼得使盡氣力將馬鈴薯搗得稀爛，白琳達小姐在蘋果醬中加糖，瑪莎擦著熱盤子，鮑伯把小提姆安置在自己身旁的一個小桌角，另外兩個小孩則幫大夥擺椅子，當然也忘不了他們自己，然後他們各自爬到椅子上睜大眼睛盯著，還把湯匙塞到嘴巴裡，免得因為等不及要吃鵝肉而尖叫起來。餐盤終於擺好，也做完了飯前禱告。接下來的一刻更是叫人屏息以待，只見克拉契太太的目光緩緩地在切肉刀上游移，準備著一刀插入鵝胸。就在她將刀插入，大夥期待已久的填料熱汁噴出來的那一剎那，桌邊響起了一陣低低的歡呼，就連小提姆也感染了兩位小兄姊的興奮情緒，用刀柄敲著桌子，有氣無力地喊了一聲「萬歲」！

這隻鵝真是前所未見。鮑伯說他就不相信世上還有人能烤出這樣一隻鵝。它的肉質鮮嫩、風味絕佳、體積龐大、價格又低，讓眾人讚不絕口。再加上蘋果醬與馬鈴薯泥，剛好足以讓全家人飽餐一頓。克拉契太太（檢查了盤子裡的一小塊骨頭後）滿心歡喜地說，甚至還有剩呢！不過每個人都吃飽了，尤其是最年幼的幾個孩子更是完全沉湎於洋蘇草與洋蔥的餘味中！這時，白琳達小姐開始換盤子，克拉契太太則獨自離開飯廳──她太緊張了，所以不想有人跟著──去將布丁起鍋，然後端上飯桌。

會不會沒有熟透？會不會一倒出來就糊了？會不會有人趁他們享用鵝肉之際，翻牆進入後院把布丁偷走了？一想到這裡，那兩個小傢伙立刻面無血色！什麼可怕的事都可能發生的！

哇！好多蒸汽！布丁起鍋了。有洗衣日那天的味道！是包在外頭那層布的關係。還有小餐館的味道，是一家緊臨著糕餅店和洗衣店的小餐館！是布丁呀。過了三十秒鐘，克拉契太太進來了：臉漲得通紅，但帶著得意的微笑，手上捧著的布丁，堅挺密實得像顆布滿斑點的砲彈，底下燃燒著四分之一品脫的白蘭地，火光耀眼，上頭則插著聖誕冬青作為點綴5。

真是個完美的布丁！鮑伯冷靜地說他認為這是他們夫妻結婚以來，妻子最大的成就。克拉契太太說既然心上的大石頭已經落了地，她不得不承認本來還擔心麵粉的份量不對。每個人都有話說，可是卻沒有人認為對他們一大家子人來說，這個布丁實在太小。這麼說或這麼想實在太不像話，只要是克拉契家的一份子便不會厚著臉皮說出這樣的話來。

最後晚餐終於結束，桌巾收起，爐床打掃乾淨，火也重新撥旺。缽裡的雜燴嘗起來恰到好處，蘋果與柳橙放上了桌，還鏟了一鏟子的栗子放到火上烤。接著克拉契一家人全都聚到火爐邊，圍成鮑伯·克拉契所謂的圓圈，其實是個半圓。鮑伯的手邊排列著家裡所有的玻璃杯，也就是兩只大杯子，和一個沒有把手的果凍杯。

用這些杯子盛裝缽裡的熱飲，味道卻也和金屬杯不相上下。鮑伯容光煥發地將熱飲盛好，火上的栗子也開始嗶嗶剝剝、劈哩啪啦響個不停。然後鮑伯舉杯祝道：

「親愛的家人，祝我們大家聖誕快樂。願上帝保佑我們！」

全家人也跟著覆頌了一遍。

「願上帝保佑我們每一個人！」小提姆最後說道。

他坐在自己的小板凳上，緊挨在父親身旁。鮑伯握著他瘦弱的小手，彷彿他愛極這個孩子，希望將他留在身邊，唯恐被人給搶走了。

「精靈，」施顧己帶著一種前所未有的興致說道：「告訴我，小提姆會不會活下去？」

「我看見在簡陋的壁爐一角，」幽靈回答道：「有一個空位子，還有一根沒有人拄著的拐杖細心地保存著。假如未來仍維持著這些影像，那麼這個孩子就會死。」

「不，不。」施顧己說：「不行呀，好心的精靈！告訴我他會逃過劫難。」

「假如未來仍維持著這些影像，」幽靈答道：「那麼我以後的任何親人都不會再見到他。那又如何呢？如果他非死不可，那還是死了的好，也可以減少過剩的人口。」

施顧己聽著精靈引述自己說過的話不禁低下頭來，感到無比後悔與悲傷。

「人啊，」幽靈說：「如果你有一顆肉做的心，而非鐵石心腸，那麼在你領悟到過剩的是什麼，過剩的又在哪裡之前，就不要再發表這種虛偽晦澀的言論了。你能決定什麼人該活，什麼人該死嗎？在老天的眼裡，你也許比千千萬萬和這個窮人家小孩一樣的人更不值得、也更沒有資格活在世上。老天爺啊！您聽聽看，葉子上的蟲兒竟然敢批評那些在泥土裡挨餓奮鬥的弟兄們，死的數量太少了！」

聽到精靈這番指責，施顧己全身戰慄，眼睛盯著地下。忽然間他聽到自己的名字，立刻抬起了雙眼。

「施顧己先生！」鮑伯說：「我們來敬施顧己先生一杯，他是賞我們這頓大餐的恩人！」

「可不是嘛！」克拉契太太臉上發紅，也大喊道：「真希望他人在這裡。我就可以將我一片感恩的心送給他享用，但願他有個好胃口，否則可能還消化不了呢！」

「親愛的，」鮑伯說：「孩子在呢……聖誕節呀。」

「當然是聖誕節囉，」她說：「我們才可能為一個像施顧己先生這麼討人厭、這麼吝嗇、這麼冷酷、這麼無情的人乾杯。他是這種人，你是知道的，鮑伯！沒有人比你更清楚了，可憐的傢伙！」

「親愛的，」鮑伯溫和地回答：「聖誕節呀。」

「看在你和聖誕節的份上，我就為他乾一杯。」克拉契太太說：「我這可不是為了他。祝他長命百歲！聖誕快樂，新年快樂！——他一定會很高興、很快樂的，我敢肯定！」

孩子們也隨著她乾杯。從剛才到現在這是他們第一個全然不帶勁的舉動。小提姆最後一個乾杯，但是他一點也不在乎。施顧己是這家人眼中的惡魔，一提到他的名字，現場便籠罩一片陰影，整整五分鐘都無法散去。

但事過境遷之後，他們比原來還要高興百倍，光是驅散了惡魔施顧己的陰影，就夠他們輕鬆的了。鮑伯‧克拉契告訴他們，他替長子彼得留意到一份工作，要是談得成，每個禮拜就能賺進五個半先令。兩個小傢伙一想到彼得成為生意人的模樣就笑個不停，而彼得藏在衣領間的臉則盯著爐火若有所思，好像正慎重地考慮著當他拿到這筆為數可觀的收入時，該做些什麼特別的投資。接著，在女帽店辛苦當學徒的瑪莎也開始訴說她的工作內容，說她得一口氣工作多少個小時，說她明天早上打算躺在床上好好地休息一下，因為明天她可以在家過節。還說她幾天前見到一位伯爵夫人和一位勛爵，說那位勛爵「大概和彼得一樣高」，彼得聽了連忙把衣領拉得老高，在場的人誰也看不到他的腦袋。

這段時間裡，栗子和熱飲遞了一圈又一圈，過了一會，小提姆為他們唱了一首歌，是關於一個在雪地中迷了路的孩子。他的聲音小得可憐，但的確唱得好極了。

這其中毫無可稱道之處。這一家人並不體面，穿著不華麗，鞋子更不可能防水，衣服都太小，而且彼得也很可能進過當鋪。但是他們很快樂，懂得感恩，彼此相處和樂，過節也很知足。當他們的影像漸漸淡去，當精靈臨行前用火炬撒下明亮的火星時，他們顯得更加愉悅，施顧己一直盯著他們不放，尤其是小提姆，直到他們完全消失為止。

此時天色漸漸暗了，大雪紛飛，施顧己和精靈沿著街道走，只見家家的廚房、客廳與各個房間裡的爐火轟然作響，火光燁然。

這一家火焰閃爍，顯然正準備著一頓豐盛的晚餐，熱騰騰的菜一道一道爭相出爐，深紅色的窗簾也即將拉攏，將寒冷與黑暗隔絕在外。

那一家，所有的孩子都跑到雪地裡，迎接已經結了婚的姊妹、兄弟、表兄弟姊妹、叔伯姑孃，而且還要第一個向他們道賀。

另一家，窗簾上映著賓客圍聚的身影。稍遠處有一群頭戴兜帽、腳上穿著毛皮靴的漂亮女孩，嘰嘰喳喳說個不停，一邊踩著輕盈的步伐走向某個鄰居家；唉，可憐那些單身漢便眼睜睜看著她們頂著紅撲撲的臉蛋往裡走——好一群狡猾迷人的女子，她們心裡可清楚得很！

路上趕著去參加聚會的人之多，會讓你以為他們到了以後，八成沒有人接待，沒想到卻是家家戶戶把壁爐燒得火光熊熊，就等著客人到來。老天哪，幽靈可真是喜出望外！它露出寬闊的胸膛，張開大大的手掌，飄啊飄，在伸手可及之處慷慨地揮灑它爽朗而天真的歡愉！眼下奔過一個點燈工人，他讓昏暗的街頭亮起點點燈火，一身的盛裝似乎也打算上哪兒過聖誕夜，而精靈一飛過，就連他也開懷大笑：只不過這名點燈工人卻想不到，這會聖誕精靈可是他唯一的伴！

忽然，幽靈事先說也沒說，他們已經站在一處空曠、荒涼的野地上，四下散置著奇形怪狀的巨岩[6]，彷彿巨人的墓地似的。到處都是水——若非寒霜將它給凍住的話，想必也是恣意奔流。地面上只長了青苔、荊豆和又粗又密的雜草。西邊的夕陽留下一道火紅的痕跡，映照著這片荒野，就像一雙慍怒的眼睛，眉頭越蹙越低，越蹙越低，最後終於隱沒在濃濃的晦暗夜色中。

「這是什麼地方？」施顧己問道。

「礦工住的地方。」精靈回答道：「他們在地心深處勞動，不過他們也知道我。你瞧！」

有一間茅屋的窗口射出亮光，他們飛快地走上前去。穿過土石牆後，他們看見一群人愉快地圍坐在閃耀的火堆邊。一對很老很老的夫妻和他們的孩子，甚至更年輕的一代，都穿著過節的衣裳盛裝打扮，神情愉快。老人正在為大夥唱一首聖誕歌，歌聲不斷被荒野上的風聲給蓋了過去，那是他小時候學會的一首很古老的歌曲，偶爾其他人也會跟著他唱；每當其他人一開口，老人就唱得更起勁、更大聲，而每當其他人閉口不唱，老人也就跟著沒了活力。

精靈沒有在此多耽擱，便要施顧己抓住它的袍子，繼續飛越荒野，急急往哪去呢？不會往大海去吧？正是往大海去。施顧己駭然回頭一看，卻見最後的一塊陸地，一整排的磈礒怪岩，已經落在背後；海水在千瘡百孔的洞穴之間翻湧、怒吼、咆哮，聲聲震耳欲聾，並企圖以洶湧澎湃的聲勢侵蝕地球。

在距離海岸幾哩遠的地方，有岩石沒入海中形成荒涼的暗礁，終年受潮水沖刷撞擊，卻有一座燈塔孤零零地立在那裡。大量的海草附著在燈塔牆根，海燕——或許也和海草一樣因風而生——在四周起落不定，就像牠們飛掠而過的海浪一般。

即使到了這裡，兩個守燈塔的人還是生了一堆火，耀眼的火光由厚厚石牆上的槍眼射出，照在令人生畏的海上。他二人坐在簡陋的桌前，握住彼此長滿厚繭的手，並以一壺水酒互道聖誕快樂。其中年紀較大的那人，臉上飽受風霜摧殘，傷疤累累，猶如一艘破船的船頭雕像，他忽然開口唱起歌來，歌聲慷慨激昂猶如一陣強風呼嘯。

幽靈又繼續前進，越過黑暗洶湧的海面，前進、前進，直到離海岸很遠——它對施顧己是這麼說的——才降落在一艘船上。他們先後站到掌舵的舵手、船首的瞭望員、值班的高級船員身邊，幽暗模糊的身影守著各自的崗位，但是每個人要不是嘴裡哼著聖誕曲子，就是想著聖誕節，再不就是低聲向同伴說著昔日聖誕節的情景，內心則充滿返家的期望。船上的每個人，無論醒著或睡著，無論好性情或壞脾氣，每到這一天說話的口氣總是比其他日子好，每個人多多少少都感染了歡樂的氣氛，還會想起遠方他所關心的人，並且知道這些人也會高高興興地想起他。

施顧己感到十分驚訝，因為當他聽著風的呼號，心想在這孤單漆黑的夜裡，航行過一道如死亡般深不可測的深淵，是多麼令人蕭然起敬的一件事！而令施顧己更加驚訝的是正當他想得入神，竟聽到一陣暢快的笑聲。令施顧己更加驚訝的是那竟然是他外甥的笑聲，他猛然發現自己已經身在一個明亮、乾爽、火光熠熠的房間裡，精靈微笑地站在他身邊，面帶讚許與和藹的神色也正看著他這個外甥。

「哈哈！」施顧己的外甥大笑：「哈哈哈！」

假如你恰巧認識一個能笑得比施顧己的外甥還痛快的人——雖然機會十分渺小——我只能說我也很想見見他。把他介紹給我吧，我很樂意與他結識。

世間事是很公平、公正、公道的，雖然疾病與悲傷會傳染，但是卻沒有什麼比笑聲與歡樂的情緒更具有感染力。施顧己的外甥笑得彎腰捧腹、搖頭晃腦，整張臉也都扭曲變形了，施顧己的甥媳婦也跟他一樣笑得好開心。而他們周遭的朋友自然也不甘示弱，哄堂大笑起來。

「哈哈！哈哈……！」

「我發誓，他真的說聖誕節是鬼扯淡！」施顧己的外甥嚷著說：「他還真是這麼想的！」

「這樣更可恥呀，弗瑞德！」施顧己的甥媳婦氣憤地說。女人哪，她們做事從來是緊追不捨，很認真的。

她長得很美，美極了。漂亮的臉蛋有兩個深深的酒渦，總是一副受驚的神色，豐潤的小嘴好像天生就是讓人親吻用的——當然也一定被親過了，下巴邊許許多多可愛的小梨渦，一笑起來便彼此相連相容不見了，還有一對陽光般燦爛的眼睛，更是在任何年輕女子的臉上都見不到。你也知道，她的整個模樣可以說是十分撩人，但也讓人看了很舒服。是呀，的確舒服到了極點！

「他是個滑稽的老傢伙，真的。」施顧己的外甥說：「他其實可以親切一點的。反正他如此無禮總會受到報應，我也不想再批評他什麼。」

「弗瑞德，我想他真的很有錢。」施顧己的甥媳婦暗示道：「至少你是這麼跟我說的。」

「那又怎麼樣呀，親愛的！」施顧己的外甥說：「他的財富對他一點用

也沒有。他既不用來做好事，也不讓自己過好日子。他甚至一想到——哈，

哈，哈！——將來受益的可能是我們，心裡就不樂意。」

「我真受不了他。」施顧己的甥媳婦說。甥媳婦的姊妹，和其他所有的女

士們也都表示同感。

「我就受得了！」施顧己的外甥說：「我覺得他很可憐，不管我怎麼試就

是無法生他的氣。他有那些奇怪的壞念頭，受害的是誰呢？到頭來總是他自

己。喏，他現在開始討厭我們，不來跟我們吃飯，結果呢？他也沒錯過什麼

豐盛的晚餐……」

「其實我倒覺得他錯過了一頓很棒的晚餐。」施顧己的甥媳婦打斷他的

話。其餘的每個人也都這麼說，他們可都有資格評斷，因為他們才剛吃過晚

飯，甜點還擺在桌上，大夥都靠攏到火邊圍在燈光下。

「大家能這麼說，我真高興。」施顧己的外甥說：「因為我對現在這些年

輕的家庭主婦實在不太有信心。你說是不是，塔波？」

塔波顯然是看上了施顧己甥媳婦的一個妹妹，因為他回答說單身漢是

沒人要的可憐蟲，沒有權利對此表示意見。一聽這話，施顧己甥媳婦的那位妹妹——是穿著蕾絲花邊、胖胖的那個，不是戴著玫瑰花的那個——臉都紅了。

「繼續說吧，弗瑞德。」施顧己的甥媳婦拍了拍手說：「話老是說一半！這傢伙真是無可救藥！」

施顧己的外甥又開始大笑起來，由於實在無法不受他感染——儘管那位胖胖的妹妹拚命地嗅著香醋——大夥還是全都跟著他笑了。

「我只是想說，」施顧己的外甥說：「他開始討厭我們，不和我們一起同樂，我想結果就是他錯過了一些歡樂時刻，而這些時刻對他一點壞處也沒有。我相信他也錯失了一些親切和善的同伴，不論是在發霉的老舊辦公室裡，或是在灰塵瀰漫的臥房裡，他都想像不出如此親善的同伴。不管他想不想要，我打算每年都給他同樣的機會，因為我同情他。他大可嘲諷聖誕節直到他死為止，可是我要向他挑戰，如果我一年又一年地去找他，好聲好氣地對他說：施顧己舅舅，你好嗎？一定能讓他改觀。就算只能讓他心血來潮留下五十鎊給他可憐的夥計，也夠好的了。而且我覺得昨天他被我打動了。」

這回輪到其他人大笑，他竟然說自己打動了施顧己。不過他是徹頭徹尾的好脾氣，雖然他們笑個不停，卻也不管他們笑什麼，反而還歡歡喜喜地遞著酒瓶，助助大夥的興。

喝過茶後，來了點音樂，因為他們這一家人都熱愛音樂，無論是合唱或輪唱，絕對都是有模有樣，尤其是塔波，他那雄渾低沉的男低音誰也比不上，而且從來也不唱得臉紅脖子粗。施顧己的甥媳婦彈得一手好豎琴；她彈了幾首曲子，其中一首簡單的小曲（真的很簡單，可能聽個兩分鐘就能跟著哼了）正是當年到學校去接施顧己那個小女孩所熟悉的旋律，過去的聖誕精靈曾經喚醒施顧己的這段回憶。當這首樂曲響起，精靈展示給他看過的事物又一一浮現腦海，他越來越軟化，並想著假如多年前能多聽聽這首曲子，也許他就能耕耘出一生中溫暖的友誼，以自己的雙手創造自己的幸福，而無須藉助於掘墓人埋葬雅各・馬利的那把鏟子了。

不過他們並不是整個晚上都唱歌。過了一會，他們開始玩起打賭的遊戲來，偶爾能當個孩子也不錯，尤其在聖誕節最恰當了，因為這一天所紀念的萬能之主不就是個小孩嗎？等等！他們玩的第一個遊戲就是捉迷藏[7]。當然是了。我可不相信塔波真的看不見，就像我也不相信他眼睛長在腳上一樣。我想他已經和施顧己的外甥串通好了，而現在的聖誕精靈也知道。看他追著那位穿蕾絲的胖妹妹跑的模樣，對於輕信人性的人真是一大侮辱。一下子撞倒火爐用具，一下子翻倒在椅子上，一下子碰到鋼琴，一下子又纏在窗簾間，無論她往哪跑，他就往哪追。他總是知道胖妹妹在哪裡，不會去抓到別人。倘若你像其中幾個人一樣故意撞上他，然後站定下來，他也會假裝企圖要捉你——簡直是侮辱你的智慧——然後立刻轉身又往胖妹妹那邊去了。她不停大喊不公平，也的確是不公平。但是到了最後，他捉到她了；儘管她迅速地在他身邊奔來跑去，蕾絲不斷窸窣作響，他還是將她逼到一個角落讓她逃無可逃。然而此時的他，行為更是惡劣。他竟然佯裝不知道是她，佯裝著必須要摸摸她的頭飾，還要捏捏她手上的戒指和她頸間的項鍊，才能確定她是誰。真是卑鄙，可恥！後來另一個人當了鬼，他們倆一塊偷偷躲在窗簾背後時，她應該也把這個想法告訴了他。

施顧己的甥媳婦沒有和大家一起玩捉迷藏，卻舒舒服服地躺在一旁角落裡的大椅子上，把腿擱在腳凳上，精靈和施顧己就站在她身後。不過她倒是加入了打賭遊戲，而且用盡了所有的字母來表達她對遊戲中情人的愛意。接著玩問答遊戲她也是高手，還把那幫姊妹們打得落花流水，施顧己的外甥不禁暗自心喜：不過塔波一定會說其他姊妹們也都很厲害。在場的大約有二十來人，不論老少都加入戰局，施顧己也不例外。因為他太過於投入，根本忘了他們聽不到自己的聲音，有時候還是大聲地說出謎底，大部分也還都猜對了，因為即使最細的針，就說是有品質保證不會在針眼處斷裂的「白教堂牌」細針好了，也比不上施顧己的敏銳：雖然他總希望自己遲鈍一點。

精靈見他心情這麼好十分歡喜，尤其當施顧己像個孩子似的哀求，希望能留下來直到所有的賓客離去後再走時，它更是以慈藹的眼光看著他。但精靈說這點它辦不到。

「又有新遊戲了。」施顧己說：「再半個小時，精靈，半個小時就好！」這個遊戲叫做「是與否」。施顧己的外甥得先想好一樣東西，讓其他人來猜，對他所問的問題，他只能回答是或否。在猛烈的質問砲火攻擊下，他透露出了他心裡想的是一種動物，還活著的動物，但卻是令人厭惡的動物，一種殘忍的動物，偶爾會高聲咆哮、低聲號叫，偶爾會說話，住在倫敦，會在街上走來走去，不是供人觀賞用的，也沒有人牽著走，不住在動物園裡，市場攤販也不曾宰殺過，不是馬，或驢子，或母牛，或公牛，或老虎，或狗，或豬，或貓，或狼。每當有人提出新的問題，這個外甥就會再次暴出如雷的笑聲，有時候實在樂不可支，還得從沙發上站起來猛頓腳。最後那位胖妹妹也和他一樣大笑起來，並大喊著說：

「我猜到了！我知道是什麼了，弗瑞德！我知道是什麼了！」

「是什麼？」弗瑞德喊道。

「是你的施—顧—己舅舅！」

自然是他了。大部分的人都一致讚嘆，只不過有幾個人提出反駁，說剛才問到「是不是狼？」的時候，答案應該是「是」，因為他否定的回答，才害得他們將施顧己先生剔除在外，倒像是他們曾經把他列入考慮似的。

「老實說，他帶給了我們不少歡樂。」弗瑞德說：「不為他乾一杯實在過意不去。現在我們手邊都有一杯溫酒，各位，敬施顧己舅舅！」

「好吧！敬施顧己舅舅！」大家齊聲喊道。

「不管他是什麼樣的人，都祝他老人家聖誕快樂，新年快樂！」施顧己的外甥說：「雖然他不領我的情，但我還是要祝福他。敬施顧己舅舅！」

施顧己舅舅在不知不覺中變得好輕鬆、好愉快，要是精靈再多給他一點時間，他也會回敬這群渾然不知他存在的同伴，並且用他們聽不見的聲音致上一篇感謝詞。然而他外甥的最後一個字才出口，整個景象便隨之消失了，他和精靈再度踏上旅程。

他們看了許多，走了很遠，造訪了不少人家，但總是快樂收場。精靈一站到病床邊，病人便開朗起來；站到異鄉的土地上，遊子便有返家的感覺；站到為謀生而奮鬥的人身旁，他們便抱著更大的希望耐心期待；站到窮人身旁，他們便富有了。在救濟院、收容所與監獄，在所有的苦難庇護所，只要自負的守門人沒有利用他短暫的小小職權將大門緊鎖，將精靈擋在門外，它便會給予祝福，並以此告誡施顧己。

倘若這只是一個夜晚的時間，可真是一個漫長的夜晚。不過施顧己卻有所懷疑，因為他們一起度過的時刻似乎濃縮了整個聖誕假期。另外很奇怪的是儘管施顧己的外貌保持不變，精靈卻變老了，很明顯地老了。施顧己注意到了這個變化，但他隻字未提，一直到他們在主顯節前夕離開一個為小孩舉辦的派對後，兩人並肩站在一處空地，施顧已再次望著精靈，才發現它的頭髮已經灰白。

「精靈的壽命這麼短嗎？」施顧已問道。

「我在這個世上的壽命非常地短。」精靈答道：「今晚就要結束了。」

「今晚！」施顧已驚叫道。

「今晚的午夜。你聽！時間就快到了。」

此時正響起十一點三刻的鐘聲。

「請恕我冒昧地問一句，」施顧已盯著精靈的袍子說道：「我看到你的衣襬下面露出一樣怪東西，那好像不是長在你身上的。是腳還是爪子呀？」

「從上頭的皮肉看起來，應該是爪子吧。」精靈悲痛地回答，「你看。」

它從長袍的褶子裡領出了兩個小孩，全身髒兮兮、衣衫襤褸、面目可憎、令人望之生厭。他們跪倒在精靈腳下，緊抓著它的衣袍。

「喂！你看這裡。看呀，往下面看！」精靈大喊。

那兩個小孩一男一女，面黃肌瘦，穿著破爛，臉上帶著慍怒、殘忍的神情，但卻也因為卑微而俯首貼耳。他們原該擁有一副充滿青春氣息的容顏，原該沾染上最清新的色彩，不料竟被一雙衰老、枯槁的手——就像歲月的手一般——摧殘、蹂躪得不成人形。原該是天使坐鎮的，不料竟成了橫眉豎眼的惡魔橫行。無論用什麼樣的神方妙法造物，也無論人類再怎麼改變、再怎麼退化、再怎麼扭曲，都及不上這怪物的一半恐怖、駭人。

施顧己大吃一驚，嚇得連連倒退。看他們就這樣出現在他面前，他試著想稱讚他們是好孩子，可是話卻硬是哽在喉頭，不願脫口造就如此一個漫天大謊。

「精靈！他們是你的孩子？」施顧已只能這麼說。

「是人類的孩子。」精靈低頭看著他們說：「他們為了逃避祖先，才會攀附著我。男孩叫『無知』，女孩叫『貧困』。要提防他們，還有他們的所有同類，尤其要提防這個男孩，因為我看見他的眉宇間寫著『劫難』，除非將它抹去，否則便在劫難逃。你們否認吧！」精靈朝著城市伸開雙臂大喊道：「儘管去污衊那些吐露事實的人吧！儘管為了爭權奪利而接受它們的存在，然後讓情況繼續惡化吧！下場自有分曉！」

「他們難道走投無路、毫無辦法了嗎？」

「現在沒有監獄嗎？」精靈最後一次拿他自己的話來反駁：「現在沒有聯合救濟院嗎？」

十二點的鐘聲響了。

施顧己四下張望，卻已經找不著精靈。最後一聲鐘響停了之後，他想起了老雅各・馬利的預言。當他抬起雙眼，便見到一個披著布袍、戴著兜帽，神情嚴肅的幽靈，像一陣霧飄過地面似的朝著他而來。

註：

1.冬青（holly）──是十九世紀時最普遍的聖誕節裝飾物。冬青具有特殊意義：象徵耶穌所戴的荊冠、復活節即將來臨。

2. 主顯節蛋糕（twelfth-night cakes）——基督徒為了慶祝第十二夜（Twelfth Night，主顯節〔Epiphany〕前夕，一月五日）而做的蛋糕，並舉行宴會度過聖誕節假期的最後一日，以紀念在耶穌誕生後，前去伯利恆（Bethlehem）拜訪的東方三賢士。

在十九世紀時，主顯節蛋糕是歡度第十二夜宴會中最引人注目的裝飾品。

3. 狄更斯的作品中經常出現「倫敦的霧」。

霧氣雖然又沈又緩，卻能滲入各個角落。雖也抵擋不了那股寒氣，再厚的呢絨與毛皮都無法保暖。儘管人蜷縮著身子，霧氣卻彷彿滲進了骨子裡，折磨得人顫抖不已，痛苦萬分。

——《老古董店》（The Old Curiosity Shop）

4. 當時幾乎沒有幾戶倫敦家庭有足夠大的烤爐可以烘烤耶誕火雞，因此大家都習慣把火雞送到麵包店去烤。當時的法律明文禁止麵包店師傅在禮拜天和耶誕節當天製作麵包。

5. 聖誕布丁（Christmas Pudding, Plum Pudding）象徵一家人在聖誕節日團結和諧的意義。

這道食譜源於十五世紀的李子濃湯（plum portage），發展到十九世紀時，這道食譜以蔗糖、果皮、肉桂、酒等製作。隨著這道聖誕布丁食譜的發明，衍生「攪動星期天」（Stir-Up Sunday）的傳統，全家人會用一把特製木匙順著攪動包在棉布裡的聖誕布丁，並許願祈求好運降臨。

將布丁端上餐桌前，要在中間刺一個洞，填滿白蘭地酒，然後點燃，在火焰的光亮中燦爛上桌。

狄更斯〈聖誕晚餐〉（A Christmas Dinner）中曾描述：「說到那頓晚宴，真是令人極其愉快——一點兒差錯也沒有。個個都情緒高漲，存心使別人高興，也讓別人使自己高興。爺爺詳盡地敘述買那隻火雞的經過，還稍微談到在昔日聖誕節買火雞的一些事，奶奶則在一旁證實著最細微的的細節。喬治叔叔講故事，切雞鴨，喝葡萄酒，和旁邊餐桌上的孩子們開玩笑，向對別人示愛的小輩們眨眨眼睛，也向被求愛的小輩們眨眨眼睛，以他的好性情和殷勤好客勁兒使所有的人都高興起來。最後一個矮胖的僕人端著一隻巨大的布丁，搖搖擺擺的走進屋來；布丁上面插著一小枝冬青，孩子們大笑大嚷，拍著胖胖的小手，短短的胖腿踢呀踢的，只有當點燃的白蘭地酒澆入聖誕布丁的驚人藝術時，小客人們熱烈的鼓掌，才比得上那股高興勁兒。接著端來的是點心——還有葡萄酒！——還有有趣的事！」

6. 奇形怪狀的巨岩——指英國西南端瓦康耳（狄更斯曾於一九四二年末，短暫居留於此處）著名的天然巨石群。

7. 捉迷藏這種遊戲最初來自於模仿祖先狩獵時的追逐景象，到了維多利亞時代，變成風行於沙龍裡的社交遊戲。

最後一個精靈

幽靈緩慢地、嚴肅地、安靜地靠近了。當它一到跟前，施顧己立刻跪下，因為精靈仿彿在它行經的空氣中，散播出幽暗與神祕。

幽靈裹著一件深黑色的長袍，蓋住了頭、臉、身形，除伸在外面的一隻手之外，其餘的什麼也看不見。因此很難從黑夜中辨識出它的形態，也很難將它與四周的黑暗區分開來。

當精靈來到施顧己身邊，他感覺得到它很高大、威嚴，而伴隨著它的神祕氣氛也讓他又敬又怕。他知道的就這麼多了，因為精靈既不說話也沒有動作。

「我眼前這位是未來的聖誕精靈嗎？」施顧己問。

精靈沒有回答，手卻往下一指。

「你要帶我去看一些尚未發生，但即將發生的事情的影像，對不對，精靈？」施顧己又問。

只見長袍上半部的縐褶繃緊了一下，好像是精靈點了點頭。這也是他得到的唯一回答。

雖然此時的施顧己已經很習慣有精靈作陪，但這個安靜無聲的形體卻讓他懼怕得底下一雙腳不停打顫，當他準備隨著它去時，竟發現自己幾乎都站不穩了。精靈注意到他的情況，便停下來讓他恢復鎮定。

不過施顧己的情形卻反而更糟。他心裡就是有一股莫名的恐懼，因為他知道在那塊黑布底下有一雙幽靈似的眼睛正凝視著自己，而他卻是無論再怎麼死命地盯，也只能看見一隻鬼手和黑壓壓的一大坨。

「未來的精靈！」他喊著：「你比其他任何一個幽靈都更叫我害怕。可是我知道你是想幫助我，而我也希望自己能脫胎換骨，所以我已經準備好帶著感恩的心與你同行。你願意和我說說話嗎？」

它沒有作聲，手則直指向前。

「帶路吧！」施顧己說：「帶路吧！夜晚很快就要過去，而時間對我來說十分寶貴，我知道。所以帶路吧，精靈！」

幽靈就像來時一樣靜悄悄地走了。施顧己跟隨著它長袍的影子，他覺得自己好像被長袍給托起，引領向前。

他們似乎不算是進城，反倒像是城市在他們周遭冒了出來，而主動將他們圍住。總之他們是到了市中心了，那是擠滿了商人的交易所。這些人有的忙進忙出，有的把口袋裡的錢幣晃得叮噹響，有的聚在一塊交談，有的不停看錶，有的則一面玩弄著大大的金印一面細心考慮，等等等等……這些畫面施顧己並不陌生。

精靈在一小群生意人旁邊停住。施顧己見它的手指向他們，便上前聽聽他們說些什麼。

「不知道。」一個下巴肥厚的大胖子說：「我什麼都不清楚。我只知道他死了。」

「什麼時候死的？」另一人問道。

「大概是昨天晚上吧。」

「唉，他出了什麼事呀？」又一人問道，同時從一個超大的鼻煙盒裡吸了一大撮鼻煙：「我還以為他永遠也不會死。」

「天曉得。」胖子打了個呵欠說。

「他那些錢怎麼處置？」一個紅臉的先生問道，他鼻頭上垂著一塊贅肉晃得好厲害，就好像火雞脖子底下的肉疣。

「我沒聽說。」肥下巴的那人說的同時又打了一個呵欠：「可能是留給公司了吧。我只知道他可沒把錢留給我。」

這句玩笑話惹得大夥都笑了。

「這場葬禮一定很寒傖。」同一人又說：「我可以發誓，我還沒聽說有誰打算去參加的。要不要我們組個志願團啊？」

「如果有午餐招待的話，我倒不介意去參加。」鼻子上長贅肉的先生說：「可是要我去，就得填飽我的肚子。」

又是一陣笑聲。

「其實，我是最興致缺缺的一個。」胖子說道：「因為我從來沒有戴過黑手套，也沒有吃過午餐。不過要是其他人有意願的話，我還是會自願去的。仔細想想，我不能不說是他最特殊的朋友，因為我們每次一碰面總會停下來聊兩句。再見囉！」

說話與聽話者慢慢散了，接著又混進其他的人群裡去。施顧己認識這些人，便望著精靈，希望它作解釋。

精靈又飄到另一條街上。它的手指指向兩名偶遇寒暄的人。施顧己再度傾聽，以為這或許能為他解開疑團。

這兩個人他也很熟。他們都是生意人：非常富有，也很具有影響力。他向來很努力想提升他們對自己的評價，當然了，這是就生意的立場而言，純粹就生意立場而言。

「你好！」一人說。

「你好！」另一人應道。

「欸！」第一人說：「他終於被撒旦給收回去了哦？」

「我也聽說了。」第二人回道：「夠冷的了，是吧？」

「聖誕節都是這樣的。我想你應該不溜冰吧？」

「不，不。還有其他事要忙呢。再見了！」

沒有再多說一個字。他們就這樣碰了面、說幾句話，然後分手。

精靈竟然會重視這番索然無味的談話，施顧己起初很感到訝異，但是他相信這其中一定隱含著某種意義，於是便開始思考了起來。他們談話的內容不太可能和他的老夥伴雅各的死有關，因為那已經是過去，而這個精靈管轄的領域卻是未來。他也想不起自己身邊有哪一個人和這番話扯得上關係。但無論這些話與誰有關，都一定有其潛在的寓意以便能讓他有所改進，因此他決定將他所聽到的每句話，他所看到的每件事都牢記在心，尤其當他自己的身影出現時更要留意觀察。因為他預料他未來的自我將會為他提示一些錯過的線索，謎底也就呼之欲出了。

他在那個地方四下張望想尋找自己的影像，但是平時屬於他的角落裡卻站著另一個人。看看時鐘的指針，通常這個時候他已經到了，但這會兒從玄關湧進的人潮當中卻沒有一個長得像他。不過他倒也不怎麼訝異，因為他已經打算改變生活方式，他以為也希望會在未來的影像中看到新的結果。

精靈站在他身旁，伸著一隻手，安靜而幽暗。當他從沉思中回過神來，忽然從精靈的手勢以及從手勢與他自身的關連當中，感覺到那雙隱形的眼睛正以銳利的目光注視著他。他不由得全身戰慄，而且覺得好冷。

他們離開了熱鬧的市街，走進市區一個偏僻的角落。施顧已從未來過這裡，可是他一眼就認出這個惡名昭彰的地方。這裡的道路又髒又窄，店鋪與住家破舊不堪，人也個個衣不蔽體，面目醜陋，醉醺醺地跋著破鞋晃蕩。這裡的巷弄與拱道就像許多下水道一樣，將噁心的氣味、穢物和人都吐到歪七扭八的街道上，整個地區瀰漫著罪惡、齷齪與悲慘。

在這個聲名狼藉的巢穴深處，有一片低矮的店鋪，屋簷雖低，店面卻直伸到街上來。這家鋪子專門收購廢鐵、破舊衣服、空瓶、骨頭和油膩的殘渣。店內的地板上一堆又一堆生銹的鑰匙、鐵釘、鐵鍊、鉸鏈、銼刀、秤盤、秤錘以及各種廢鐵。幾乎無人想探究的祕密就在這堆積如山的破舊衣物中，在這腐敗的脂肪山與這骨頭堆成的墳穴裡滋生、藏匿。在這些交易貨品當中，有一隻用舊磚頭堆砌成的炭爐，炭爐旁坐著一個年近七十、頭髮花白的老傢伙。他將一面用零零碎碎的破布拼成、已經發霉發臭的帘子，掛在一根繩子上，以遮擋外頭的冷空氣，一邊滿足而悠閒地抽著煙斗。

正當施顧已與幽靈來到此人面前之際，恰巧有一個婦人揹著一大包東西悄悄地進入店中。但她才剛踏進門口，就有另外一個同樣揹著一大包東西的婦人也進來了，而她身後則緊跟著一個穿著一身褪色黑衣的男人。這男人看到她們嚇了一大跳，而她們認出了對方也同樣吃驚。就在他們目瞪口呆的當兒，抽煙斗的老人迎上前來，他們三人才暴出了笑聲。

「清潔婦第一個到！」首先進來的婦人喊道：「洗衣婦第二個到，葬儀社的人第三個到。你瞧瞧，老喬，這可巧了！我們可不是說好一起來的！」

「在這裡碰頭是再好不過了。」老喬從嘴裡抽出煙斗說：「進客廳來吧。妳早就在這裡進出過了，是吧，另外兩人也都不是第一次來。等一下，我關個門。哎喲！真是刺耳！我看哪，這裡頭就沒有哪塊廢鐵比這扇門的鉸鏈生銹得更厲害，也沒有哪根骨頭比我這把老骨頭還老的。哈哈！我們都沒有幹錯行，都配得挺好的。進客廳來。進客廳來吧。」

客廳就是破布帘後面的那塊地方。老人拿起一根用來壓住樓梯口地毯的舊木棍將炭火耙攏，接著用煙桿壓了壓冒煙的燈芯（因為已經入夜了），之後，又把煙斗含進嘴裡。

在他做這些事的同時，已經說過話的婦人將布包甩在地板上，跨開雙腳便一屁股往矮凳上坐，她兩隻手臂交抱放在膝頭，然後用一種挑釁的態度看著另外兩人。

「這又怎麼樣！這又怎麼樣呢，狄柏太太？」婦人說：「每個人都有權利為自己打算。他向來都是這樣！」

「的確是如此！」洗衣婦說：「沒有人比得上他。」

「那就別站在那兒乾瞪眼啊，妳這個女人，好像怕了似的。誰會知道呢？我想，我們總不至於互揭瘡疤吧？」

「當然不會！」狄柏太太和那個男人異口同聲地說：「我們可不想這麼做。」

「那好極了！」婦人嚷道：「這就行了。不過就這麼一點東西，會給誰造成損失？死人更無所謂了，對吧？」

「的確如此。」狄柏太太笑著說。

「這個壞心又吝嗇的老傢伙，」婦人又接著說：「如果他死後還想保住這些東西，活著的時候怎麼不有人性一點？要是他有點人性，死神找上門的時候就會有人在他身邊照顧他，也不至於孤孤單單地嚥下最後一口氣。」

「這話說得再中肯不過了。」狄柏太太說：「這是他的報應。」

「真希望報應還能再重一點，」婦人應道：「我說真的，要是我還能多拿走一點，我就會讓他有多一點的報應。把布包打開吧，老喬，幫我估個價。

多少你就直說了。我不怕當第一個，也不怕他們看。我想我們在這裡碰面之前，就都知道大夥會這麼做了。這不是什麼罪過。把布包打開吧，老喬。」

不過她的兩位友人立刻客氣地制止了他。穿著褪色黑衣的男人首先挺身而出，拿出了他搜刮來的財物；東西並不多，全部也只有一兩枚印章、一個鉛筆盒、一對袖口的鈕釦，和一枚沒什麼價值的胸針。老喬一一地檢視、估價，然後用粉筆將每樣東西的價錢寫在牆上，最後東西都看完了，他才全部加總。

「你的就值這麼多。」老喬說：「就算讓我下油鍋，我也不會再多添一分錢。下一個輪到誰？」

下一個是狄柏太太。床單和毛巾、幾件衣服、兩支舊式的銀湯匙、一把糖夾，和幾雙靴子。老喬也和剛才一樣將她的金額記在牆上。

「我給女人的價錢總是太高。這是我的老毛病，我也就毀在這一點。」老喬說：「妳的東西值這麼多。如果妳想跟我討價還價，要我多出一分錢，我可就不這麼慷慨了，還要再扣妳半克朗。」

「現在可以掏開我的布包了，喬。」第一位婦人說。

喬雙膝著地，解起布包更方便一點，解開許許多多個結之後，從裡頭拉出來一捲又黑、又厚、又沉的東西。

「這是什麼玩意？」喬說：「床帷！」

「欸！」婦人回道，一面笑一面抱著胳臂往前傾：「床帷！」

「該不會是他還躺在床上，妳就把布幔、環鉤什麼的都拆下來了吧？」喬說。

「我是啊。」婦人應道：「怎麼不行呢？」

「妳天生就有發財命，當然一定會發財囉。」喬說。

「喬，對他這種人，我向你保證，只要我一伸手就能拿到的東西，就絕對不會手下留情。」婦人冷冷地回答：「喂，別把油滴到毛毯上了。」

「是他的毛毯？」喬問道。

「不然你以為會是誰的？」婦人反問：「我敢說呀，就算沒有這些毯子，他也不會凍著的。」

「他不是得什麼傳染病死的吧？嗯？」老喬停下手邊的活兒，抬起頭來問道。

「這個你不用擔心。」婦人回說：「我可沒有那麼喜歡陪著他，要是他真得了傳染病，我才不會為了這些東西留在他身邊磨蹭。噢！那件襯衫你儘管檢查，保證找到你眼睛痠痛也找不到一個破洞，或是磨損的地方。那是他最好的一件，也真的挺不錯的，要不是被我拿來，可就浪費了。」

「為什麼說是浪費？」老喬問道。

「因為就會讓他穿著下葬了呀。」婦人笑著回答：「就有人笨到做這種事，還好又讓我給脫下來了。這個時候還不穿白布襯衣，那白布豈不是一點用也沒有？何況也挺合身的。反正穿那件也不會比穿別的難看。」

施顧己聽著這段對話，越聽越害怕。這幾個人圍坐在他們的戰利品旁邊，只有老人的那盞燈發出微弱的光線，他看著他們感到無比憎惡與鄙夷，此時就算是一群可恨的魔鬼商討著要把屍體給賣掉，都還不至於讓他如此深惡痛絕。

「哈，哈！」當老喬拿出一只裝滿錢幣的法蘭絨袋，在地上開始一一數錢要付給他們時，第一名婦人大笑起來：「你瞧，結果就是這樣！他在世的時候把每個人都嚇跑了，死了以後卻讓我們撿到便宜！哈，哈，哈！」

「精靈！」施顧己從頭到腳抖個不停：「我懂了，我懂了。我可能會跟這個可憐的人同樣下場。我的人生正朝著那個方向走。老天爺，多可怕呀！」

此時景象突然變了，他的手幾乎碰到了一張床，他不禁嚇得縮起身來。

那張床光禿禿的，沒有床帷、床罩，床上有一條破破的床單，底下好像躺了什麼，雖然不聲不響的，卻以一種恐怖的語言宣示著它的存在。

雖然施顧己忍不住內心的衝動而東張西望，急著想知道這是什麼樣一個房間，可是房內實在太暗，暗得看不清任何細節。一絲黯淡的光線從外頭直接射在床上，那上頭躺著一具屍體，被洗劫一空，孤苦無依，無人看顧，無人料理，無人悲傷哭泣。

施顧己瞄了幽靈一眼。只見它的手定定地指著屍體的頭部；床單只是胡亂蓋著，只要施顧己手指稍微往上一掀，臉就會整個露出來。他心裡想著，覺得易如反掌，也渴望著要去做，但是他卻無力掀開那塊布，就如同他無力驅走身邊的幽靈。

呵，冷冰冰、頑固、可怕的死神，在此設起你的祭壇，用你所能支配的一切恐懼來裝飾吧……因為這正是你所擅長的！可是面對一個曾經被愛、被崇仰、被尊敬的人的人頭時，你卻無法迫使任何一根頭髮屈服於你的威嚇之下，也無法塑造任何可憎的面貌。如今他的手也許沉重，一鬆開便會垂下，心跳與脈搏或許也停了，但是那雙手曾經開啟、慷慨而真誠，心曾經勇敢、熱情而溫柔，脈搏裡也曾流著人的熱血。刺吧，幽靈，刺吧！你將會見到他的善行從傷口湧出，為世界散播永恆的生命！

在施顧己的耳邊並沒有什麼聲音說出這些話，可是當他看著床上時確實聽見了。他心想假如這個人當下死而復生，他的第一個念頭會是什麼？是貪念，是商場上的激烈競爭，還是為利益斤斤計較？這些念頭可真是讓他走得好風光呀！

他躺在空空暗暗的屋子裡，沒有一個男人，或女人，或小孩說「他曾經這樣或那樣地對我好，為了感念他說過的一句好話，所以我也要對他好」。有一隻貓用爪子搔著門板，爐灶底下傳來老鼠咬東西的聲音。這些傢伙在死人的房間裡想做什麼，為什麼如此浮躁、騷動？施顧己不敢多想。

「精靈！」他說：「這個地方太可怕了。離開之後，我一定會記取教訓的，相信我。我們走吧！」

然而幽靈的手還是動也不動地指著死者的頭。

「我明白你的意思。」施顧己回答道：「如果我做得到，我也會去做。可是我無能為力呀，精靈，我無能為力。」

精靈似乎又抬起眼睛看著他。

「這城裡如果有誰的情緒因為此人的死而受影響，」施顧己十分痛苦地說：「求求你讓我見見他吧，精靈！」

精靈像展翅似的拉開黑袍遮住他，過了一會黑袍撤去後，眼前出現的是白晝裡的一個房間，裡面有一位母親和她的幾個孩子。

她在等人，而且等得焦急萬分。因為她在房裡踱來踱去，一聽到聲響就驚跳起來，還不時看看窗外，瞄瞄時鐘，雖然試著想做點針線活卻是徒然，而且幾乎無法忍受孩子們嬉鬧的聲音。

最後，她期待許久的敲門聲終於響起，她立刻衝到門邊迎接丈夫。她的丈夫年紀雖輕，一張臉卻顯得憔悴而沮喪。此時他臉上有一種很奇特的表情，好像是打心底高興卻又感到羞恥，因此極力地想克制住。

他走到火邊坐下，吃起了特地為他留的晚餐。當妻子（在沉默了很長一段時間之後）小聲地問他有什麼特別消息，他似乎尷尬得不知如何回答。

「是好消息，」她問道：「還是壞消息？」──也算是幫幫他。

「壞消息。」他回答道。

「我們真的沒有希望了？」

「不，卡洛琳，我們還有希望。」

「他要是大發慈悲，才會有希望！」她驚詫地說：「要是真有這樣的奇蹟發生，還有什麼是沒希望的呢！」

「他沒有大發慈悲。」她丈夫說：「他死了。」

倘使她的臉蛋不會撒謊，那麼她的確是一個性情溫厚、極能容忍的人；不過聽到這個消息，她心裡可真感謝上帝，而她也雙手合十老實地說了出來。片刻過後，她感到過意不去便祈求上帝原諒，然而先前那才是她內心裡真正的情緒。

「我昨晚向妳提過，我去找他想請他寬限一個禮拜，結果遇到一個喝得半醉的女人，我當時以為她說的話只是他用來躲避我的藉口，沒想到竟然是真的。那個時候，他不只是病得很重，而且已經快死了。」

「那他的債權移轉給誰？」

「不知道。反正到時候我們也已經有錢了，就算沒有不至於那麼倒楣，又碰到一個和他一樣無情的新債主。我們今晚可以放鬆心情睡個好覺了，卡洛琳！」

是的。雖然有些不忍，但是心情確實是輕鬆了。孩子們安安靜靜圍著聽他們說話，雖然似懂非懂，但臉色也變得明朗了。這個人的死讓這家人更加快樂！精靈唯一能讓他看見因為這件事所引發的情緒，竟然是一種喜悅之情。

「讓我看看對死者的一點憐憫吧。」施顧己說：「否則我們剛剛離開的那個黑暗房間，將會永遠印在我的腦海呀，精靈。」

幽靈引領著他穿過幾條他熟悉的街道，他們沿路走著，施顧己則一面左顧右盼地尋找自己，卻是怎麼也找不著。他們走進可憐的鮑伯‧克拉契的家──他之前已經來過──看見母親和孩子圍坐在火爐邊。

安安靜靜的。沒有一點聲音。吵鬧不休的兩個小傢伙此時竟像雕像一般，動也不動地坐在角落裡，抬頭望著彼得，而彼得手裡則拿著一本書。母親和兩個女兒正忙著做針線活，她們當然更是安靜了！

「耶穌便叫一個小孩子來，使他站在他們當中。」

施顧已在哪聽到這句話的？不是在夢中。一定是他和精靈跨過門檻時，那個男孩大聲念出來的。他怎麼不繼續念下去呢？

母親將手裡的活放到桌上，用手摀住臉。

「這顏色太刺眼了。」她說。

顏色？啊，可憐的小提姆！

「現在又好一點了。」克拉契太太說：「在燭光下做活，眼睛好吃力，再怎麼說我也不能讓爸爸回來的時候，看見我兩眼疲憊。他回家的時間快到了。」

「都已經過了。」彼得將書闔上，回答道：「我總覺得他這幾天走路的速度比以前慢。」

大夥再度陷入沉默。最後克拉契太太以沉穩而愉快的聲音——這中間只結巴了一次——說道：

「我知道他以前扛著……我知道他以前扛著小提姆，走得很快呢。」

「我也知道！」彼得喊道：「常常的事。」

「我也知道！」另一人大叫道。其他人也都這麼喊著。

「可是提姆很輕很輕，」她低著頭做活，又接著說：「爸爸又那麼愛他，所以沒有問題……沒有問題。是爸爸回來了！」

她趕忙迎上前去，小鮑伯跟著走了進來，頸子上圍著圍巾──可憐的傢伙，他可真是少不了它。他的茶已經泡好放在壁爐邊架上熱著，大家都爭先恐後地要替他倒。然後兩個小傢伙爬上他的膝頭，各自將小臉頰貼到他的臉上，彷彿告訴他說：「爸爸，不要擔心，不要難過！」

鮑伯面對他們，神情十分愉快，與其他家人聊天時也顯得很快活。他看看桌上的女紅，稱讚妻子與女兒的手藝又巧又快。應該早在禮拜天之前就能完成了，他說。

「禮拜天！這麼說你今天去了，鮑伯？」妻子說。

「是的，親愛的。」鮑伯回答道：「真希望妳也去了。看看那麼油綠綠的一個地方，對妳有好處的。不過以後妳還有很多機會。我答應他禮拜天會去那兒走走。我的小小孩!」鮑伯哭道:「我的孩子呀!」

他瞬間崩潰了,再也忍不住傷心。如果他能忍得住,他和他的孩子也許會更疏遠。

他離開客廳爬到樓上的房間去,房裡燈光耀眼,還布置著聖誕飾物。孩子身旁擺了一張椅子,上頭還留著最近有人坐過的痕跡。可憐的鮑伯坐到椅子上,沉思了一會,待情緒恢復之後,親了親孩子的小臉蛋。他默默接受了事實,再度快快樂樂地下樓去了。

他們聚在火邊談天,母女三人依然繼續做著手邊的活。鮑伯告訴他們施顧己先生的外甥有多麼仁慈,他只見過他一面,那天他們在街上相遇,他見鮑伯有一點——「只是一點點沮喪而已」,鮑伯說,便問他發生了什麼事。「我從來沒有見過講話這麼和氣的人,於是便告訴了他。他說:『克拉契先生,我由衷地為你感到難過,也由衷地為你賢慧的妻子感到難過。』真是怪了,我就想不通他怎麼會知道。」

「知道什麼?」

「親愛的,知道什麼?」

「知道妳是個賢慧的妻子呀。」鮑伯答道。

「這個大家都知道！」彼得說。

「孩子，說得好！」鮑伯喊道：「但願如此吧。他說：『由衷地為你賢慧的妻子感到難過。如果我能幫上什麼忙的話，這是我的地址，請你來找我。』他一面說一面遞給了我他的名片。其實，倒不是他能幫我們什麼，而是他那親切和藹的態度，讓人覺得舒服極了。就好像他認識我們的小提姆，所以也和我們一樣難過似的。」

「我想他一定是個好人！」克拉契太太說。

「妳要是當面和他說過話，」鮑伯答道：「妳還會更加肯定。要是他替彼得找一份更好的工作，我也不會覺得訝異，我說真的。」

「彼得，你聽聽。」克拉契太太說。

「這樣一來，」其中一個女兒喊道：「彼得就會開始交朋友，然後成家了。」

「你少胡說。」彼得咧著嘴反駁道。

「孩子，」鮑伯說：「雖然時間還早，但總有那麼一天。不過不管我們如何分開，何時分開，我相信都不會有人忘記可憐的小提姆，或是忘記我們之間這第一次的分別，對不對？」

「絕對不會的，父親！」大家都高聲喊道。

「而且我知道，」鮑伯說：「我知道當我們想起他雖然只是小小年紀，卻那麼能夠容忍又那麼溫和，我們之間就決不會爭吵，否則就等於忘記小提姆了。」

「是的，父親，我們絕對不會！」大家又高聲喊道。

「我太高興了！」小鮑伯說：「我太高興了！」

克拉契太太親了他，女兒親了他，兩個小傢伙親了他，彼得則和他握了握手。小提姆的靈魂呀，你童稚的本質來自於上帝！

「精靈，」施顧己說：「我有個感覺，我們分別的時刻就要到了。告訴我，我們剛才看到躺在床上的死者是誰？」

未來的聖誕精靈又像先前一樣將他送到商人經常出沒的地方──雖然時間不一樣，但他心想：其實後來的這些影像似乎並無先後順序之分，只不過都屬於未來罷了──然而，他還是沒有看見自己。事實上，精靈並未在任何地方稍作停留，彷彿急著趕往目的地似的往前直行，一直到施顧己哀求它耽擱一下。

「我們匆忙趕過的這條巷子，」施顧己說：「是我工作的地方，而且已經很長的時間。我看見辦公室了，就讓我瞧瞧我將來是什麼樣子吧。」

精靈停了下來，手卻指著另一處。

「辦公室在那邊，」施顧己大叫：「你為什麼指向其他地方？」

那手指毫不動搖，依然沒有改變方向。

施顧己連忙跑到辦公室的窗口，往內一看，裡面還是一間辦公室，但卻不是他的。家俱換了，坐在椅子上的人也不是他。幽靈還是像原來那樣地指著。

他又回到幽靈身邊，不明白自己為什麼不在，又會跑到哪去。他最後陪著精靈來到一扇鐵柵門前，他先停下來四下看了看才走進去。

那是一個教堂墓地。這麼說，那個不知名的悲慘人士就躺在這片土地下。這是個名副其實的墓地。四周的房子將整個地方團團圍住，遍地雜草，象徵的是草木的死氣而非生機；地下擠滿了屍體，土壤肥沃得已達飽和。一個名副其實的墓地！

精靈站在墳墓間，朝其中一座指著。施顧己顫抖著向那座墳走去。幽靈還是保持原來那副模樣，可是在那嚴肅的外表下他彷彿看見了新的意圖，不禁感到懼怕。

「在我走向你所指的那座墓碑之前，」施顧己說：「回答我一個問題。這些是未來確定會發生的影像，或者只是可能發生的影像？」

幽靈還是往下指著它身邊的那座墳。

「從人一生的過程便可以預見他的下場，」施顧己說：「假如過程持續不變，便躲不過那樣的命運。但是假如中途轉向了，那麼結果也會不同。你讓我看到的情形便是如此，對不對？」

精靈依然不動如山。

施顧己悄悄地走到它身邊，全身不住發抖。順著手指的方向看去，他發現那塊荒涼的墓碑上刻著自己的名字……「艾布內茲‧施顧己」。

「躺在床上的那個人就是我？」他跪倒在地，哭喊道。

精靈的手指從墓碑移向他，之後又移了回去。

「不，精靈！不要，不要！」

手指還是沒動。

「精靈呀！」他緊緊抓住精靈的袍子大喊著：「你聽我說！我已經不是從前的我。如今與你們交流過，我決不會變成我原本要成為的那個人。如果已經毫無希望，又何必讓我看這一切呢？」

那隻手終於微微地動了一下。

「好精靈，」他拜倒在它跟前，繼續又說：「你的內心也憐憫我，為我求情。答應我吧，我只要有了不一樣的生活，我就能改變你所展現的這些幻影！」

它仁慈的手顫抖著。

「我會打心裡尊敬聖誕，也會盡量一年到頭保持這份心。我會活在過去、現在與未來，我會將這三個精靈時時牢記在心，我不會對他們的教訓置之不理。噢，請你告訴我說我可以抹去這塊石碑上的刻文吧！」

施顧己激動地握住幽靈的手。精靈想掙脫，但他苦苦哀求之際卻生出極大的力量，把那隻手抓得緊緊的。但精靈的力量畢竟更大，還是甩開了他。

當施顧己最後一次合掌懇求改變自己的命運時，他看見精靈的兜帽與衣袍開始變形，慢慢地變小、變矮、變瘦，最後成了一根床柱。

註：

1. 狄更斯在《博茲札記》(Sketches by Boz, 1836) 一書中描寫七晷區 (Seven Dials) 的街道（七晷區的街道十九世紀時位在科芬園 (Covent Garden) 劇院區的後方，是當時的貧民窟）。狄更斯在造訪過一間舊衣店（販售剛過世之人的衣服與財物）後，寫道：「這些衣服上頭刻寫著這個人的一生，明明白白地，就好像當著我們的面用複寫紙拷貝下來的一樣。」

尾聲

5

沒錯！而且是他自己的床柱。床是他的，房間是他的。而最令他快活的是，就連將來的時間也是他的，可以讓他好好改過自新！

「我會活在過去、現在與未來！」施顧已翻下床來，嘴裡重覆著這些話：「我會將這三個精靈時時牢記在心。雅各·馬利呀！感謝老天和聖誕節！老雅各，我可是跪著這麼說的，跪著說的！」

他一心想著重新做人，情緒過於激動，喊啞了的嗓子幾乎已經不聽指揮。因為與精靈爭辯時哭得淒慘，此時他的臉上仍涕泗縱橫。

「沒有被拆掉，」施顧已一面床帷挽進臂彎裡，叫喊著：「沒有被拆掉，環鉤什麼的都沒拆。東西都還在，我也還在，本來會發生的事情的幻影是可以消除的。一定會消除的，我知道一定會的。」

這時候他一面說一面玩弄著他的衣服，一忽兒翻面，一忽兒倒穿，拉拉扯扯，到處亂扔，讓一件件衣服也都跟著他發癲。

「我該怎麼辦哪？」施顧己又哭又笑地大喊，手裡抓起兩只長襪當海蛇，自己則成了拉奧孔……「我輕飄飄得像羽毛，快樂得像天使，快活得像小學生，頭暈得像喝醉了酒。祝大家聖誕快樂！祝全世界的人新年快樂。喂！喲呵！喂！」

他蹦蹦跳跳地進了客廳，現在站在那裡，喘得上氣不接下氣。

「那是裝麥片粥的燉鍋！」施顧己喊道，接著又開始在壁爐邊雀躍蹦跳起來：「那是門，雅各‧馬利的靈魂就是從這裡進來的！現在的聖誕精靈就坐在那個角落！還有窗戶，我就在窗戶邊看見遊蕩的靈魂！一切都沒事，一切都是真的，一切都過去了。哈哈哈！」

的確，對一個多年來疏於練習的人而言，好個燦爛的笑聲，好個驚天動地的笑聲。這一笑也開啟了好長、好長一串的爽朗笑聲！

「我不知道今天的日子是幾號！」施顧己說：「我不知道我和精靈們在一起多久。我什麼都不知道。我可真像個小嬰兒。無所謂，我不在乎，我寧願當個小嬰兒。喂！喲呵！喂！」

他正欣喜若狂之際，被教堂的鐘聲給打斷了，那是他所聽過最洪亮的聲響。鏗鏗鏘，叮叮噹。叮叮噹，鏗鏗鏘！噢，太美妙，太美妙了！

他奔到窗邊，打開窗子，頭探了出去。沒有濃霧，沒有煙靄，晴朗、明亮、歡愉、繁忙、寒冷，一種像吹著笛子讓人血液隨之起舞的冷。金黃的陽光，美好的天空，清新甜美的空氣，歡樂的鐘聲。噢，太美妙，太美妙了！

「今天幾號啊？」施顧己朝底下一名全身盛裝的小男孩喊道，那男孩大概是偷溜進來瞧瞧究竟的。

「嗄？」小男孩大吃了一驚，應道。

「今天是幾號，小乖？」施顧己說。

「今天？」小男孩回答道：「聖誕節啊。」

「今天是聖誕節！」施顧己自言自語：「我沒有錯過。精靈在一個晚上就全辦好了。它們想怎麼做就怎麼做。當然是這樣，當然是這樣了。喂，小乖！」

「什麼事！」小男孩應道。

「隔兩條街的轉角有一間賣雞鴨的店，你知道嗎？」施顧己問道。

「當然知道了。」小孩回答。

「真聰明！」施顧己說：「太聰明了！你知不知道本來掛在店門口那隻得獎的火雞賣掉沒有？不是那隻小火雞，是大的那隻。」

「就是跟我一樣大的那隻？」男孩反問。

「真是個討人喜歡的孩子！」施顧己說：「跟你說話可真有趣。是的，孩子！」

「現在還掛在那裡。」男孩回答。

「是嗎？」施顧己說：「去幫我買回來。」

「你騙人！」男孩嚷道。

「不，不，」施顧己說：「我說真的。你去幫我買，然後請店裡的人帶著火雞過來，我再告訴他們要送到哪裡去。你跟夥計一起回來，我給你一個先令。要是五分鐘以內回來，我就給你半個克朗！」

男孩立刻像飛箭一樣射了出去。看來這個弓箭手出手一定很穩，才能讓箭飛得這麼快。

「我要把火雞送給鮑伯・克拉契！」施顧己喃喃說道，他搓搓手，忍不住笑了起來：「他不會知道是誰送的。這火雞可比小提姆大兩倍呢。把火雞送給鮑伯，就連喬‧米勒 2 也沒開過這麼大的玩笑！」

他寫地址的時候手不停抖著，不過終於還是寫好了，然後便到樓下打開大門，等著雞肉店的夥計到來。當他站在那裡等候時，忽然瞥見了門環。

「只要我活著一天，就會好好愛護它！」施顧己拍拍門環喊道：「以前我幾乎沒有注意過它。這張臉的表情多真誠！太棒了，這個門環！——火雞來了。嗨！你好呀！聖誕快樂！」

好大的一隻火雞！牠一定從來也沒站起來過，否則那雙腳恐怕不到一分鐘，就會像封蠟棒一樣折斷了。

「怎麼可能扛著這隻火雞上坎登鎮？」施顧己說：「非得叫一輛車不可。」

他說這話時忍不住竊笑，付火雞的錢時忍不住竊笑，付車費時忍不住竊笑，賞錢給小男孩時也忍不住竊笑，直到他氣喘吁吁地重新坐到椅子上，才終於放聲大笑，直笑到眼淚都流出來了。

刮鬍子可不是件簡單的事，因為他的手依然抖得厲害，而且刮鬍子必須專心，光是不手舞足蹈都還不夠。但是就算他把鼻尖給削了下來，他頂多貼上一塊膠布，興致依然不減。

施顧己把自己打扮得光鮮體面，終於上街去了。此時已是人潮洶湧，就如同他和現在的聖誕精靈所看見的情景一般，他將手揹在背後，笑容滿面地看著每一個人。總而言之，他的態度實在太親切了，有三四個好心情的人忍不住便對他說：「先生，早啊！祝你聖誕快樂！」後來施顧己還常說，他聽過那麼多愉快的聲音裡頭，就數這些聽起來最悅耳。

沒走多遠，迎面便來了一位身材高大的中年人，正是前一天到他辦公室來，並說「施顧己與馬利商號，是吧？」的那個人。一想到他們相遇時，這位老紳士會怎麼看他，施顧己便感到心如刀割，但是他知道自己眼前該走的路，也就不再遲疑。

「親愛的先生。」施顧己加快腳步向前，雙手握住老先生的手說道：「你好嗎？但願你們昨天有豐富的收穫。你人真是太好了。祝你聖誕快樂！」

「施顧己先生嗎？」

「是的。」施顧己說：「正是我本人，你恐怕不太想聽到這個名字吧。

請容我向你致歉。不知道是不是能請你……」這時施顧己附到他耳邊把話說完。

「老天哪！」那位先生彷彿窒息似的大喊道：「我親愛的施顧己先生，你說的是真的？」

「麻煩你了，」施顧己說：「一分錢也不會少。這裡頭有大部分都是我拖欠下來的，我不騙你。你能幫我這個忙嗎？」

「敬愛的先生，」另一人握著他的手說：「我真不知道該說什麼，你這麼地慷……」

「請你什麼都不用說了。」施顧己打斷他：「請來找我。你會來找我吧？」

「我會的！」老先生喊道，他顯然是一定會做到。

「謝謝。」施顧己說：「非常感謝。無任感激。上帝保佑你！」

他上了教堂，又在街上四處閒晃，看著路人熙來攘往，摸摸孩子的頭，向乞丐問問好，探頭看看各家的廚房，抬頭看看各戶的窗子，一切都讓他感到愉快。他從來沒想到散個步——或是做任何事——能為自己帶來這麼多的快樂。到了下午，他往外甥的家裡走去。

他在門口來來回回走了十幾趟，才終於鼓起勇氣上前敲門，不過他是衝上去敲的門。

「妳的主人在家嗎？」施顧己向女孩問道。一個漂亮的女孩！漂亮極了！

「在。」

「那麼他人呢？」施顧己說。

「他和太太在飯廳裡。我先帶你上樓去，請跟我來。」

「謝謝。他認識我的。」施顧己說，手則已經按在飯廳的門把上了：「我直接進去就好了，孩子。」

他輕輕地開了門，側著臉從門縫探頭進去。大夥都盯著桌子看（上頭已經擺得琳琅滿目），這些年輕主婦對這類的細節總是很挑剔，總希望沒有任何瑕疵。

「弗瑞德！」施顧己叫道。

我的天哪，他的甥媳婦嚇得跳了起來！施顧己一時忘了她正抬著腳坐在角落裡，否則他無論如何是不會這麼做的。

「哎呀！」弗瑞德嚷著：「看看是誰來了？」

「是我，你的施顧己舅舅。我是來吃晚飯的。我可以進來嗎，弗瑞德？」

他可以進來嗎！他的手沒有被握斷已經很幸運了。不到五分鐘，馬上有了賓至如歸的感覺，再也沒有人比他們更熱情的了。他的甥媳婦和他所看到的一模一樣。塔波來了，他也一樣。美好的聚會，美好的遊戲，美好的和諧，美好的幸福！每個人都來了，也都一樣。胖妹妹來了，她也一樣。

不過，第二天一早他就進了辦公室。他可是真早。要是他能第一個到，把遲到的鮑伯‧克拉契逮個正著，該有多好！他一心這麼盤算著。

他辦到了。他可不是辦到了嗎！大鐘敲了九響。鮑伯沒來。十五分鐘過了。他整整遲到了十八分鐘又三十秒。施顧己坐在裡面，將門大開，那麼鮑伯進油槽間時他才能看得見。

他開門之前已經將帽子脫下，圍巾也拿掉了。一眨眼就坐到椅子上，筆飛快地動了起來，彷彿想趕上九點似的。

「喂！」施顧己盡量裝出平日的聲音咆哮道：「你搞什麼？這個時候才

「實在很抱歉，老闆。」鮑伯說：「我的確是遲到了。」

「遲到？」施顧己重覆著說：「是啊，我想也是。麻煩你過來一下。」

「老闆，一年不過就這麼一次。」鮑伯從油槽間走出來，哀求道：「以後絕對不會了。昨天晚上我玩得太高興了。」

「我告訴你吧，老弟。」施顧己說：「我不能讓事情再這樣下去。所以呢……」他從椅子上跳起來，在鮑伯的腰間猛然一按，鮑伯腳下不穩搖搖晃晃地又跌進了油槽間裡，只聽施顧己接著說道：「所以我打算加你的薪！」

鮑伯聽了全身發抖，不覺往桌上的直尺挪近了些。有那麼一剎那，他真想拿起長尺將施顧己敲昏，然後抓住他，到巷子外向人求助，請他們拿一件綁瘋子用的緊身衣來。

「聖誕快樂呀，鮑伯！」施顧己拍拍他的背，用一種毋庸置疑的熱忱對他說：「鮑伯，我的好夥計，我要給你一個這麼多年以來最快樂的聖誕節！我要加你的薪，還要盡力幫助你辛苦的家人，今天下午我們就準備一鉢熱騰騰的果子酒慶祝聖誕，順便談談你的事！先把火生起來，再去買一簍煤炭，然

來！」

後要認真做事再去做吧，鮑伯‧克拉契！」

施顧己做的比說的還多。他一切都做到了，甚至還要更多，他可以說是小提姆——他沒有死——的第二個父親。他變成了一個好朋友、好老闆、好人，而且是這個古老的倫敦城，也是這個古老的世界上任何古老的城鄉市鎮都難得一見的好人。有些人看見他的轉變都笑了，他便任由他們去笑，一點也不在意。因為他的智慧告訴他這世上的一切好事，一開始總會受到無止盡的嘲笑，而他也知道這些人反正都是盲目的，因此——他心想——盲人笑瞇了眼睛的模樣總比其他不討喜的模樣來得好吧。他暗自笑到心坎裡去……對他來說這也就很夠了。

他沒有再與精靈打過交道，並且從此完全戒除，可是大家總是說：如果世界上有誰懂得如何慶祝聖誕，那自然是非他莫屬。但願別人也能這麼評價我們，我們每一個人！最後套一句小提姆說的話：願上帝保佑我們，我們每一個人！

註：

1. 拉奧孔——出現於希臘神話「特洛伊戰爭」中的悲劇人物。特洛伊城的祭司拉奧孔（Laocoön）極力阻止特洛伊人將藏有希臘士兵的木馬拖入城內，因而觸怒希臘保護神雅典娜，拉奧孔父子三人被雅典娜所派出的巨蛇活活咬死。

2. 喬·米勒——Joe Miller，一七九三年，英國有個叫喬·莫特里（John Motteley）的人編寫了一本名為「Joe Miller's Jest Book」的笑話集。並假托當時目不識丁的喜劇演員喬瑟夫·米勒（Joseph Miller）之名出版。喬·米勒（Joe Miller）一詞比喻老掉牙的笑話。

Marley's Ghost.

Scrooge's third Visitor.

讀者回函卡

感謝您對本館的支持，為加強對您的服務，請填妥此卡，免付郵資寄回，可隨時收到本館最新出版訊息，及享受各種優惠。

■ 姓名：＿＿＿＿＿＿＿＿＿＿＿＿　性別：□ 男 □ 女

■ 出生日期：＿＿＿＿年＿＿＿＿月＿＿＿＿日

■ 職業：□學生 □公務(含軍警) □家管 □服務 □金融 □製造 □資訊 □大眾傳播 □自由業 □農漁牧 □退休 □其他

■ 學歷：□高中以下（含高中）□大專 □研究所（含以上）

■ 地址：＿＿＿＿＿＿＿＿＿＿＿＿＿＿＿＿＿＿＿＿＿

■ 電話：(H)＿＿＿＿＿＿＿＿＿＿ (O)＿＿＿＿＿＿＿＿＿

■ E-mail：＿＿＿＿＿＿＿＿＿＿＿＿＿＿＿＿＿＿＿＿＿

■ 購買書名：＿＿＿＿＿＿＿＿＿＿＿＿＿＿＿＿＿＿＿

■ 您從何處得知本書？

　　□網路 □DM廣告 □報紙廣告 □報紙專欄 □傳單
　　□書店 □親友介紹 □電視廣播 □雜誌廣告 □其他

■ 您喜歡閱讀哪一類別的書籍？

　　□哲學‧宗教 □藝術‧心靈 □人文‧科普 □商業‧投資
　　□社會‧文化 □親子‧學習 □生活‧休閒 □醫學‧養生
　　□文學‧小說 □歷史‧傳記

■ 您對本書的意見？（A/滿意 B/尚可 C/須改進）

　　內容＿＿＿＿＿編輯＿＿＿＿校對＿＿＿＿翻譯＿＿＿＿

　　封面設計＿＿＿＿價格＿＿＿＿其他＿＿＿＿＿＿＿＿

■ 您的建議：＿＿＿＿＿＿＿＿＿＿＿＿＿＿＿＿＿＿＿

※ 歡迎您隨時至本館網路書店發表書評及留下任何意見

臺灣商務印書館　The Commercial Press, Ltd.

台北市100重慶南路一段三十七號　電話：(02)23115538
讀者服務專線：0800056196　傳真：(02)23710274
郵撥：0000165-1號　E-mail：ecptw@cptw.com.tw
網路書店網址：http://www.cptw.com.tw　部落格：http://blog.yam.com/ecptw
臉書：http://facebook.com/ecptw

100台北市重慶南路一段37號

臺灣商務印書館　收

對摺寄回，謝謝！

傳統現代　並翼而翔

Flying with the wings of tradtion and modernity.

經典|小說06

聖誕頌歌
A Christmas Carol

作　　　者：狄更斯(Charles Dickens)
譯　　　者：顏湘如
發 行 人：施嘉明
總 編 輯：方鵬程
叢書主編：葉幗英
責任編輯：王窈姿
美術設計：吳郁婷
校　　　對：王窈姿
出 版 者：臺灣商務印書館股份有限公司
　　　　　The Commercial Press, Ltd.
地　　　址：台北市中正區重慶南路一段37號
電　　　話：(02)23713712
讀者專線：0800056196
郵政劃撥：0000165-1
E-mail：ecptw@cptw.com.tw
網　　　址：www.cptw.com.tw
初版一刷：2012年12月
定　　　價：新台幣280元
局版北市業第993號

ISBN 978-957-05-2789-6

聖誕頌歌 / 狄更斯(Charles Dickens)
　著；顏湘如譯. -- 初版. -- 臺北市：臺灣商
務，2012. 12
　　面；　　公分. --（經典小說）
　譯自：A Christmas Carol
　ISBN 978-957-05-2789-6（平裝）

873.57　　　　　　　　　　　101022094

A CHRISTMAS CAROL

IN PROSE

BEING

A GHOST STORY OF CHRISTMAS

BY

CHARLES DICKENS

PREFACE

I HAVE endeavoured in this Ghostly little book, to raise the Ghost of an Idea, which shall not put my readers out of humour with themselves, with each other, with the season, or with me. May it haunt their houses pleasantly, and no one wish to lay it.

Their faithful Friend and Servant,

C. D.

December, 1843.

CONTENTS

STAVE I

MARLEY'S GHOST······5

STAVE II

THE FIRST OF THE THREE SPIRITS······34

STAVE III

THE SECOND OF THE THREE SPIRITS······61

STAVE IV

THE LAST OF THE SPIRITS······95

STAVE V

THE END OF IT······118

MARLEY'S GHOST

M arley was dead, to begin with. There is no doubt whatever about that. The register of his burial was signed by the clergyman, the clerk, the undertaker, and the chief mourner. Scrooge signed it. And Scrooge's name was good upon 'Change, for anything he chose to put his hand to. Old Marley was as dead as a door-nail.

Mind! I don't mean to say that I know, of my own knowledge, what there is particularly dead about a door-nail. I might have been inclined, myself, to regard a coffin-nail as the deadest piece of ironmongery in the trade. But the wisdom of our ancestors is in the simile; and my unhallowed hands shall not disturb it, or the Country's done for. You will therefore permit me to repeat, emphatically, that Marley was as dead as a door-nail.

Scrooge knew he was dead? Of course he did. How could it be otherwise? Scrooge and he were partners for I don't know how many years. Scrooge was his sole executor, his sole administrator, his sole assign, his sole residuary legatee, his sole friend, and sole

mourner. And even Scrooge was not so dreadfully cut up by the sad event, but that he was an excellent man of business on the very day of the funeral, and solemnised it with an undoubted bargain.

The mention of Marley's funeral brings me back to the point I started from. There is no doubt that Marley was dead. This must be distinctly understood, or nothing wonderful can come of the story I am going to relate. If we were not perfectly convinced that Hamlet's Father died before the play began, there would be nothing more remarkable in his taking a stroll at night, in an easterly wind, upon his own ramparts, than there would be in any other middle-aged gentleman rashly turning out after dark in a breezy spot—say Saint Paul's Churchyard, for instance—literally to astonish his son's weak mind.

Scrooge never painted out Old Marley's name. There it stood, years afterwards, above the warehouse door: Scrooge and Marley. The firm was known as Scrooge and Marley. Sometimes people new to the business called Scrooge Scrooge, and sometimes Marley, but he answered to both names. It was all the same to him.

Oh! But he was a tight-fisted hand at the grindstone, Scrooge! a squeezing, wrenching, grasping, scraping, clutching, covetous, old sinner! Hard and sharp as flint, from which no steel had ever

struck out generous fire; secret, and self-contained, and solitary as an oyster. The cold within him froze his old features, nipped his pointed nose, shrivelled his cheek, stiffened his gait; made his eyes red, his thin lips blue; and spoke out shrewdly in his grating voice. A frosty rime was on his head, and on his eyebrows, and his wiry chin. He carried his own low temperature always about with him; he iced his office in the dog-days; and didn't thaw it one degree at Christmas.

External heat and cold had little influence on Scrooge. No warmth could warm, no wintry weather chill him. No wind that blew was bitterer than he, no falling snow was more intent upon its purpose, no pelting rain less open to entreaty. Foul weather didn't know where to have him. The heaviest rain, and snow, and hail, and sleet, could boast of the advantage over him in only one respect. They often "came down" handsomely, and Scrooge never did.

Nobody ever stopped him in the street to say, with gladsome looks, "My dear Scrooge, how are you? When will you come to see me?" No beggars implored him to bestow a trifle, no children asked him what it was o'clock, no man or woman ever once in all his life inquired the way to such and such a place, of Scrooge. Even the blind men's dogs appeared to know him; and when they saw him coming on, would tug their owners into doorways and

up courts; and then would wag their tails as though they said, "No eye at all is better than an evil eye, dark master!"

But what did Scrooge care? It was the very thing he liked. To edge his way along the crowded paths of life, warning all human sympathy to keep its distance, was what the knowing ones call "nuts" to Scrooge.

Once upon a time—of all the good days in the year, on Christmas Eve—old Scrooge sat busy in his counting-house. It was cold, bleak, biting weather: foggy withal: and he could hear the people in the court outside go wheezing up and down, beating their hands upon their breasts, and stamping their feet upon the pavement stones to warm them. The city clocks had only just gone three, but it was quite dark already—it had not been light all day—and candles were flaring in the windows of the neighbouring offices, like ruddy smears upon the palpable brown air. The fog came pouring in at every chink and keyhole, and was so dense without, that although the court was of the narrowest, the houses opposite were mere phantoms. To see the dingy cloud come drooping down, obscuring everything, one might have thought that Nature lived hard by, and was brewing on a large scale.

The door of Scrooge's counting-house was open that he might keep his eye upon his clerk, who in a dismal little cell beyond, a

sort of tank, was copying letters. Scrooge had a very small fire, but the clerk's fire was so very much smaller that it looked like one coal. But he couldn't replenish it, for Scrooge kept the coal-box in his own room; and so surely as the clerk came in with the shovel, the master predicted that it would be necessary for them to part. Wherefore the clerk put on his white comforter, and tried to warm himself at the candle; in which effort, not being a man of a strong imagination, he failed.

"A merry Christmas, uncle! God save you!" cried a cheerful voice. It was the voice of Scrooge's nephew, who came upon him so quickly that this was the first intimation he had of his approach.

"Bah!" said Scrooge, "Humbug!"

He had so heated himself with rapid walking in the fog and frost, this nephew of Scrooge's, that he was all in a glow; his face was ruddy and handsome; his eyes sparkled, and his breath smoked again.

"Christmas a humbug, uncle!" said Scrooge's nephew. "You don't mean that, I am sure?"

"I do," said Scrooge. "Merry Christmas! What right have you to be merry? What reason have you to be merry? You're poor enough."

"Come, then," returned the nephew gaily. "What right have

9

you to be dismal? What reason have you to be morose? You're rich enough."

Scrooge having no better answer ready on the spur of the moment, said, "Bah!" again; and followed it up with "Humbug."

"Don't be cross, uncle!" said the nephew.

"What else can I be," returned the uncle, "when I live in such a world of fools as this? Merry Christmas! Out upon merry Christmas! What's Christmas time to you but a time for paying bills without money; a time for finding yourself a year older, and not an hour richer; a time for balancing your books and having every item in 'em through a round dozen of months presented dead against you? If I could work my will," said Scrooge indignantly, "every idiot who goes about with 'Merry Christmas' on his lips, should be boiled with his own pudding, and buried with a stake of holly through his heart. He should!"

"Uncle!" pleaded the nephew.

"Nephew!" returned the uncle, sternly, "keep Christmas in your own way, and let me keep it in mine."

"Keep it!" repeated Scrooge's nephew. "But you don't keep it."

"Let me leave it alone, then," said Scrooge. "Much good may it do you! Much good it has ever done you!"

"There are many things from which I might have derived good, by which I have not profited, I dare say," returned the

nephew; "Christmas among the rest. But I am sure I have always thought of Christmas time, when it has come round—apart from the veneration due to its sacred name and origin, if anything belonging to it can be apart from that—as a good time; a kind, forgiving, charitable, pleasant time; the only time I know of, in the long calendar of the year, when men and women seem by one consent to open their shut-up hearts freely, and to think of people below them as if they really were fellow-passengers to the grave, and not another race of creatures bound on other journeys. And therefore, uncle, though it has never put a scrap of gold or silver in my pocket, I believe that it *has* done me good, and *will* do me good; and I say, God bless it!"

The clerk in the tank involuntarily applauded. Becoming immediately sensible of the impropriety, he poked the fire, and extinguished the last frail spark for ever.

"Let me hear another sound from *you*," said Scrooge, "and you'll keep your Christmas by losing your situation! You're quite a powerful speaker, sir," he added, turning to his nephew. "I wonder you don't go into Parliament."

"Don't be angry, uncle. Come! Dine with us to-morrow."

Scrooge said that he would see him—yes, indeed he did. He went the whole length of the expression, and said that he would see him in that extremity first.

"But why?" cried Scrooge's nephew. "Why?"

"Why did you get married?" said Scrooge.

"Because I fell in love."

"Because you fell in love!" growled Scrooge, as if that were the only one thing in the world more ridiculous than a merry Christmas. "Good afternoon!"

"Nay, uncle, but you never came to see me before that happened. Why give it as a reason for not coming now?"

"Good afternoon," said Scrooge.

"I want nothing from you; I ask nothing of you; why cannot we be friends?"

"Good afternoon," said Scrooge.

"I am sorry, with all my heart, to find you so resolute. We have never had any quarrel, to which I have been a party. But I have made the trial in homage to Christmas, and I'll keep my Christmas humour to the last. So A Merry Christmas, uncle!"

"Good afternoon!" said Scrooge.

"And A Happy New Year!"

"Good afternoon!" said Scrooge.

His nephew left the room without an angry word, notwithstanding. He stopped at the outer door to bestow the greetings of the season on the clerk, who, cold as he was, was warmer than Scrooge; for he returned them cordially.

"There's another fellow," muttered Scrooge; who overheard him: "my clerk, with fifteen shillings a week, and a wife and family, talking about a merry Christmas. I'll retire to Bedlam."

This lunatic, in letting Scrooge's nephew out, had let two other people in. They were portly gentlemen, pleasant to behold, and now stood, with their hats off, in Scrooge's office. They had books and papers in their hands, and bowed to him.

"Scrooge and Marley's, I believe," said one of the gentlemen, referring to his list. "Have I the pleasure of addressing Mr. Scrooge, or Mr. Marley?"

"Mr. Marley has been dead these seven years," Scrooge replied. "He died seven years ago, this very night."

"We have no doubt his liberality is well represented by his surviving partner," said the gentleman, presenting his credentials.

It certainly was; for they had been two kindred spirits. At the ominous word "liberality," Scrooge frowned, and shook his head, and handed the credentials back.

"At this festive season of the year, Mr. Scrooge," said the gentleman, taking up a pen, "it is more than usually desirable that we should make some slight provision for the poor and destitute, who suffer greatly at the present time. Many thousands are in want of common necessaries; hundreds of thousands are in want of common comforts, sir."

"Are there no prisons?" asked Scrooge.

"Plenty of prisons," said the gentleman, laying down the pen again.

"And the Union workhouses?" demanded Scrooge. "Are they still in operation?"

"They are. Still," returned the gentleman, "I wish I could say they were not."

"The Treadmill and the Poor Law are in full vigour, then?" said Scrooge.

"Both very busy, sir."

"Oh! I was afraid, from what you said at first, that something had occurred to stop them in their useful course," said Scrooge. "I'm very glad to hear it."

"Under the impression that they scarcely furnish Christian cheer of mind or body to the multitude," returned the gentleman, "a few of us are endeavouring to raise a fund to buy the Poor some meat and drink, and means of warmth. We choose this time, because it is a time, of all others, when Want is keenly felt, and Abundance rejoices. What shall I put you down for?"

"Nothing!" Scrooge replied.

"You wish to be anonymous?"

"I wish to be left alone," said Scrooge. "Since you ask me what I wish, gentlemen, that is my answer. I don't make merry myself

at Christmas and I can't afford to make idle people merry. I help to support the establishments I have mentioned—they cost enough; and those who are badly off must go there."

"Many can't go there; and many would rather die."

"If they would rather die," said Scrooge, "they had better do it, and decrease the surplus population. Besides—excuse me—I don't know that."

"But you might know it," observed the gentleman.

"It's not my business," Scrooge returned. "It's enough for a man to understand his own business, and not to interfere with other people's. Mine occupies me constantly. Good afternoon, gentlemen!"

Seeing clearly that it would be useless to pursue their point, the gentlemen withdrew. Scrooge resumed his labours with an improved opinion of himself, and in a more facetious temper than was usual with him.

Meanwhile the fog and darkness thickened so, that people ran about with flaring links, proffering their services to go before horses in carriages, and conduct them on their way. The ancient tower of a church, whose gruff old bell was always peeping slily down at Scrooge out of a gothic window in the wall, became invisible, and struck the hours and quarters in the clouds, with tremulous vibrations afterwards, as if its teeth were chattering in

its frozen head up there. The cold became intense. In the main street, at the corner of the court, some labourers were repairing the gas-pipes, and had lighted a great fire in a brazier, round which a party of ragged men and boys were gathered: warming their hands and winking their eyes before the blaze in rapture. The water-plug being left in solitude, its overflowings sullenly congealed, and turned to misanthropic ice. The brightness of the shops where holly sprigs and berries crackled in the lamp heat of the windows, made pale faces ruddy as they passed. Poulterers' and grocers' trades became a splendid joke: a glorious pageant, with which it was next to impossible to believe that such dull principles as bargain and sale had anything to do. The Lord Mayor, in the stronghold of the mighty Mansion House, gave orders to his fifty cooks and butlers to keep Christmas as a Lord Mayor's household should; and even the little tailor, whom he had fined five shillings on the previous Monday for being drunk and blood-thirsty in the streets, stirred up to-morrow's pudding in his garret, while his lean wife and the baby sallied out to buy the beef.

Foggier yet, and colder! Piercing, searching, biting cold. If the good Saint Dunstan had but nipped the Evil Spirit's nose with a touch of such weather as that, instead of using his familiar weapons, then indeed he would have roared to lusty purpose.

The owner of one scant young nose, gnawed and mumbled by the hungry cold as bones are gnawed by dogs, stooped down at Scrooge's keyhole to regale him with a Christmas carol: but at the first sound of—

"God bless you, merry gentleman!
May nothing you dismay!"

Scrooge seized the ruler with such energy of action, that the singer fled in terror, leaving the keyhole to the fog and even more congenial frost.

At length the hour of shutting up the counting-house arrived. With an ill-will Scrooge dismounted from his stool, and tacitly admitted the fact to the expectant clerk in the Tank, who instantly snuffed his candle out, and put on his hat.

"You'll want all day to-morrow, I suppose?" said Scrooge.

"If quite convenient, sir."

"It's not convenient," said Scrooge, "and it's not fair. If I was to stop half-a-crown for it, you'd think yourself ill used, I'll be bound?"

The clerk smiled faintly.

"And yet," said Scrooge, "you don't think *me* ill-used, when I pay a day's wages for no work."

The clerk observed that it was only once a year.

"A poor excuse for picking a man's pocket every twenty-fifth of December!" said Scrooge, buttoning his great-coat to the chin. "But I suppose you must have the whole day. Be here all the earlier next morning."

The clerk promised that he would; and Scrooge walked out with a growl. The office was closed in a twinkling, and the clerk, with the long ends of his white comforter dangling below his waist (for he boasted no great-coat), went down a slide on Cornhill, at the end of a lane of boys, twenty times, in honour of its being Christmas-eve, and then ran home to Camden Town as hard as he could pelt, to play at blindman's-buff.

Scrooge took his melancholy dinner in his usual melancholy tavern; and having read all the newspapers, and beguiled the rest of the evening with his banker's book, went home to bed. He lived in chambers which had once belonged to his deceased partner. They were a gloomy suite of rooms, in a lowering pile of building up a yard, where it had so little business to be, that one could scarcely help fancying it must have run there when it was a young house, playing at hide-and-seek with other houses, and have forgotten the way out again. It was old enough now, and dreary enough, for nobody lived in it but Scrooge, the other rooms being all let out as offices. The yard was so dark that even

Scrooge, who knew its every stone, was fain to grope with his hands. The fog and frost so hung about the black old gateway of the house, that it seemed as if the Genius of the Weather sat in mournful meditation on the threshold.

Now, it is a fact, that there was nothing at all particular about the knocker on the door, except that it was very large. It is also a fact, that Scrooge had seen it, night and morning, during his whole residence in that place; also that Scrooge had as little of what is called fancy about him as any man in the City of London, even including—which is a bold word—the corporation, aldermen, and livery. Let it also be borne in mind that Scrooge had not bestowed one thought on Marley, since his last mention of his seven-years' dead partner that afternoon. And then let any man explain to me, if he can, how it happened that Scrooge, having his key in the lock of the door, saw in the knocker, without its undergoing any intermediate process of change—not a knocker, but Marley's face.

Marley's face. It was not in impenetrable shadow as the other objects in the yard were, but had a dismal light about it, like a bad lobster in a dark cellar. It was not angry or ferocious, but looked at Scrooge as Marley used to look: with ghostly spectacles turned up on its ghostly forehead. The hair was curiously stirred, as if by breath or hot air; and, though the eyes were wide open, they were

perfectly motionless. That, and its livid colour, made it horrible; but its horror seemed to be in spite of the face and beyond its control, rather than a part of its own expression.

As Scrooge looked fixedly at this phenomenon, it was a knocker again.

To say that he was not startled, or that his blood was not conscious of a terrible sensation to which it had been a stranger from infancy, would be untrue. But he put his hand upon the key he had relinquished, turned it sturdily, walked in, and lighted his candle.

He *did* pause, with a moment's irresolution, before he shut the door; and he *did* look cautiously behind it first, as if he half expected to be terrified with the sight of Marley's pigtail sticking out into the hall. But there was nothing on the back of the door, except the screws and nuts that held the knocker on, so he said "Pooh, pooh!" and closed it with a bang.

The sound resounded through the house like thunder. Every room above, and every cask in the wine-merchant's cellars below, appeared to have a separate peal of echoes of its own. Scrooge was not a man to be frightened by echoes. He fastened the door, and walked across the hall, and up the stairs: slowly too: trimming his candle as he went.

You may talk vaguely about driving a coach and six up a good

old flight of stairs, or through a bad young Act of Parliament; but I mean to say you might have got a hearse up that staircase, and taken it broadwise, with the splinter-bar towards the wall and the door towards the balustrades: and done it easy. There was plenty of width for that, and room to spare; which is perhaps the reason why Scrooge thought he saw a locomotive hearse going on before him in the gloom. Half-a-dozen gas-lamps out of the street wouldn't have lighted the entry too well, so you may suppose that it was pretty dark with Scrooge's dip.

Up Scrooge went, not caring a button for that. Darkness is cheap, and Scrooge liked it. But before he shut his heavy door, he walked through his rooms to see that all was right. He had just enough recollection of the face to desire to do that.

Sitting-room, bed-room, lumber-room. All as they should be. Nobody under the table, nobody under the sofa; a small fire in the grate; spoon and basin ready; and the little saucepan of gruel (Scrooge had a cold in his head) upon the hob. Nobody under the bed; nobody in the closet; nobody in his dressing-gown, which was hanging up in a suspicious attitude against the wall. Lumber-room as usual. Old fire-guard, old shoes, two fish-baskets, washing-stand on three legs, and a poker.

Quite satisfied, he closed his door, and locked himself in; double-locked himself in, which was not his custom. Thus secured

21

Stave I

against surprise, he took off his cravat; put on his dressing-gown and slippers, and his nightcap; and sat down before the fire to take his gruel.

It was a very low fire indeed; nothing on such a bitter night. He was obliged to sit close to it, and brood over it, before he could extract the least sensation of warmth from such a handful of fuel. The fire-place was an old one, built by some Dutch merchant long ago, and paved all round with quaint Dutch tiles, designed to illustrate the Scriptures. There were Cains and Abels, Pharaoh's daughters, Queens of Sheba, Angelic messengers descending through the air on clouds like feather-beds, Abrahams, Belshazzars, Apostles putting off to sea in butter-boats, hundreds of figures to attract his thoughts; and yet that face of Marley, seven years dead, came like the ancient Prophet's rod, and swallowed up the whole. If each smooth tile had been a blank at first, with power to shape some picture on its surface from the disjointed fragments of his thoughts, there would have been a copy of old Marley's head on every one.

"Humbug!" said Scrooge; and walked across the room.

After several turns, he sat down again. As he threw his head back in the chair, his glance happened to rest upon a bell, a disused bell, that hung in the room, and communicated for some purpose now forgotten with a chamber in the highest story of

the building. It was with great astonishment, and with a strange, inexplicable dread, that as he looked, he saw this bell begin to swing. It swung so softly in the outset that it scarcely made a sound; but soon it rang out loudly, and so did every bell in the house.

This might have lasted half a minute, or a minute, but it seemed an hour. The bells ceased as they had begun, together. They were succeeded by a clanking noise, deep down below; as if some person were dragging a heavy chain over the casks in the wine-merchant's cellar. Scrooge then remembered to have heard that ghosts in haunted houses were described as dragging chains.

The cellar-door flew open with a booming sound, and then he heard the noise much louder on the floors below; then coming up the stairs; then coming straight towards his door.

"It's humbug still!" said Scrooge. "I won't believe it."

His colour changed though, when, without a pause, it came on through the heavy door, and passed into the room before his eyes. Upon its coming in, the dying flame leaped up, as though it cried, "I know him! Marley's Ghost!" and fell again.

The same face: the very same. Marley in his pigtail, usual waistcoat, tights, and boots; the tassels on the latter bristling, like his pigtail, and his coat-skirts, and the hair upon his head. The chain he drew was clasped about his middle. It was long,

and wound about him like a tail; and it was made (for Scrooge observed it closely) of cash-boxes, keys, padlocks, ledgers, deeds, and heavy purses wrought in steel. His body was transparent; so that Scrooge, observing him, and looking through his waistcoat, could see the two buttons on his coat behind.

Scrooge had often heard it said that Marley had no bowels, but he had never believed it until now.

No, nor did he believe it even now. Though he looked the phantom through and through, and saw it standing before him; though he felt the chilling influence of its death-cold eyes; and marked the very texture of the folded kerchief bound about its head and chin, which wrapper he had not observed before; he was still incredulous, and fought against his senses.

"How now!" said Scrooge, caustic and cold as ever. "What do you want with me?"

"Much!"—Marley's voice, no doubt about it.

"Who are you?"

"Ask me who I *was*."

"Who *were* you then?" said Scrooge, raising his voice. "You're particular, for a shade." He was going to say "to a shade," but substituted this, as more appropriate.

"In life I was your partner, Jacob Marley."

"Can you—can you sit down?" asked Scrooge, looking

doubtfully at him.

"I can."

"Do it, then."

Scrooge asked the question, because he didn't know whether a ghost so transparent might find himself in a condition to take a chair; and felt that in the event of its being impossible, it might involve the necessity of an embarrassing explanation. But the ghost sat down on the opposite side of the fire-place, as if he were quite used to it.

"You don't believe in me," observed the Ghost.

"I don't," said Scrooge.

"What evidence would you have of my reality beyond that of your senses?"

"I don't know," said Scrooge.

"Why do you doubt your senses?"

"Because," said Scrooge, "a little thing affects them. A slight disorder of the stomach makes them cheats. You may be an undigested bit of beef, a blot of mustard, a crumb of cheese, a fragment of an underdone potato. There's more of gravy than of grave about you, whatever you are!"

Scrooge was not much in the habit of cracking jokes, nor did he feel, in his heart, by any means waggish then. The truth is, that he tried to be smart, as a means of distracting his own attention,

and keeping down his terror; for the spectre's voice disturbed the very marrow in his bones.

To sit staring at those fixed glazed eyes in silence, for a moment, would play, Scrooge felt, the very deuce with him. There was something very awful, too, in the spectre's being provided with an infernal atmosphere of its own. Scrooge could not feel it himself, but this was clearly the case; for though the Ghost sat perfectly motionless, its hair, and skirts, and tassels, were still agitated as by the hot vapour from an oven.

"You see this toothpick?" said Scrooge, returning quickly to the charge, for the reason just assigned; and wishing, though it were only for a second, to divert the vision's stony gaze from himself.

"I do," replied the Ghost.

"You are not looking at it," said Scrooge.

"But I see it," said the Ghost, "notwithstanding."

"Well!" returned Scrooge, "I have but to swallow this, and be for the rest of my days persecuted by a legion of goblins, all of my own creation. Humbug, I tell you—humbug!"

At this the spirit raised a frightful cry, and shook its chain with such a dismal and appalling noise, that Scrooge held on tight to his chair, to save himself from falling in a swoon. But how much greater was his horror, when the phantom taking off the bandage round its head, as if it were too warm to wear in-doors, its lower

jaw dropped down upon its breast!

Scrooge fell upon his knees, and clasped his hands before his face.

"Mercy!" he said. "Dreadful apparition, why do you trouble me?"

"Man of the worldly mind!" replied the Ghost, "do you believe in me or not?"

"I do," said Scrooge. "I must. But why do spirits walk the earth, and why do they come to me?"

"It is required of every man," the Ghost returned, "that the spirit within him should walk abroad among his fellow-men, and travel far and wide; and if that spirit goes not forth in life, it is condemned to do so after death. It is doomed to wander through the world—oh, woe is me!—and witness what it cannot share, but might have shared on earth, and turned to happiness!"

Again the spectre raised a cry, and shook its chain and wrung its shadowy hands.

"You are fettered," said Scrooge, trembling. "Tell me why?"

"I wear the chain I forged in life," replied the Ghost. "I made it link by link, and yard by yard; I girded it on of my own free-will, and of my own free-will I wore it. Is its pattern strange to *you*?"

Scrooge trembled more and more.

"Or would you know," pursued the Ghost, "the weight and

length of the strong coil you bear yourself? It was full as heavy and as long as this, seven Christmas Eves ago. You have laboured on it, since. It is a ponderous chain!"

Scrooge glanced about him on the floor, in the expectation of finding himself surrounded by some fifty or sixty fathoms of iron cable: but he could see nothing.

"Jacob," he said, imploringly. "Old Jacob Marley, tell me more. Speak comfort to me, Jacob!"

"I have none to give," the Ghost replied. "It comes from other regions, Ebenezer Scrooge, and is conveyed by other ministers, to other kinds of men. Nor can I tell you what I would. A very little more is all permitted to me. I cannot rest, I cannot stay, I cannot linger anywhere. My spirit never walked beyond our counting-house—mark me!—in life my spirit never roved beyond the narrow limits of our money-changing hole; and weary journeys lie before me!"

It was a habit with Scrooge, whenever he became thoughtful, to put his hands in his breeches pockets. Pondering on what the Ghost had said, he did so now, but without lifting up his eyes, or getting off his knees.

"You must have been very slow about it, Jacob," Scrooge observed, in a business-like manner, though with humility and deference.

"Slow!" the Ghost repeated.

"Seven years dead," mused Scrooge. "And travelling all the time!"

"The whole time," said the Ghost. "No rest, no peace. Incessant torture of remorse."

"You travel fast?" said Scrooge.

"On the wings of the wind," replied the Ghost.

"You might have got over a great quantity of ground in seven years," said Scrooge.

The Ghost, on hearing this, set up another cry, and clanked its chain so hideously in the dead silence of the night, that the Ward would have been justified in indicting it for a nuisance.

"Oh! captive, bound, and double-ironed," cried the phantom, "not to know, that ages of incessant labour by immortal creatures, for this earth must pass into eternity before the good of which it is susceptible is all developed. Not to know that any Christian spirit working kindly in its little sphere, whatever it may be, will find its mortal life too short for its vast means of usefulness. Not to know that no space of regret can make amends for one life's opportunity misused! Yet such was I! Oh! such was I!"

"But you were always a good man of business, Jacob," faltered Scrooge, who now began to apply this to himself.

"Business!" cried the Ghost, wringing its hands again.

"Mankind was my business. The common welfare was my business; charity, mercy, forbearance, and benevolence were, all, my business. The dealings of my trade were but a drop of water in the comprehensive ocean of my business!"

It held up its chain at arm's length, as if that were the cause of all its unavailing grief, and flung it heavily upon the ground again.

"At this time of the rolling year," the spectre said, "I suffer most. Why did I walk through crowds of fellow-beings with my eyes turned down, and never raise them to that blessed Star which led the Wise Men to a poor abode? Were there no poor homes to which its light would have conducted *me*!"

Scrooge was very much dismayed to hear the spectre going on at this rate, and began to quake exceedingly.

"Hear me!" cried the Ghost. "My time is nearly gone."

"I will," said Scrooge. "But don't be hard upon me! Don't be flowery, Jacob! Pray!"

"How it is that I appear before you in a shape that you can see, I may not tell. I have sat invisible beside you many and many a day."

It was not an agreeable idea. Scrooge shivered, and wiped the perspiration from his brow.

"That is no light part of my penance," pursued the Ghost. "I am here to-night to warn you, that you have yet a chance and

hope of escaping my fate. A chance and hope of my procuring, Ebenezer."

"You were always a good friend to me," said Scrooge. "Thank'ee!"

"You will be haunted," resumed the Ghost, "by Three Spirits."

Scrooge's countenance fell almost as low as the Ghost's had done.

"Is that the chance and hope you mentioned, Jacob?" he demanded, in a faltering voice.

"It is."

"I—I think I'd rather not," said Scrooge.

"Without their visits," said the Ghost, "you cannot hope to shun the path I tread. Expect the first to-morrow, when the bell tolls One."

"Couldn't I take 'em all at once, and have it over, Jacob?" hinted Scrooge.

"Expect the second on the next night at the same hour. The third upon the next night when the last stroke of Twelve has ceased to vibrate. Look to see me no more; and look that, for your own sake, you remember what has passed between us!"

When it had said these words, the spectre took its wrapper from the table, and bound it round its head, as before. Scrooge knew this, by the smart sound its teeth made, when the jaws were

31

brought together by the bandage. He ventured to raise his eyes again, and found his supernatural visitor confronting him in an erect attitude, with its chain wound over and about its arm.

The apparition walked backward from him; and at every step it took, the window raised itself a little, so that when the spectre reached it, it was wide open. It beckoned Scrooge to approach, which he did. When they were within two paces of each other, Marley's Ghost held up its hand, warning him to come no nearer. Scrooge stopped.

Not so much in obedience, as in surprise and fear: for on the raising of the hand, he became sensible of confused noises in the air; incoherent sounds of lamentation and regret; wailings inexpressibly sorrowful and self-accusatory. The spectre, after listening for a moment, joined in the mournful dirge; and floated out upon the bleak, dark night.

Scrooge followed to the window: desperate in his curiosity. He looked out.

The air was filled with phantoms, wandering hither and thither in restless haste, and moaning as they went. Every one of them wore chains like Marley's Ghost; some few (they might be guilty governments) were linked together; none were free. Many had been personally known to Scrooge in their lives. He had been quite familiar with one old ghost, in a white waistcoat, with a

monstrous iron safe attached to its ankle, who cried piteously at being unable to assist a wretched woman with an infant, whom it saw below, upon a doorstep. The misery with them all was, clearly, that they sought to interfere, for good, in human matters, and had lost the power for ever.

Whether these creatures faded into mist, or mist enshrouded them, he could not tell. But they and their spirit voices faded together; and the night became as it had been when he walked home.

Scrooge closed the window, and examined the door by which the Ghost had entered. It was double-locked, as he had locked it with his own hands, and the bolts were undisturbed. He tried to say "Humbug!" but stopped at the first syllable. And being, from the emotion he had undergone, or the fatigues of the day, or his glimpse of the Invisible World, or the dull conversation of the Ghost, or the lateness of the hour, much in need of repose; went straight to bed, without undressing, and fell asleep upon the instant.

STAVE II

THE FIRST OF THE THREE SPIRITS

W hen Scrooge awoke, it was so dark, that looking out of bed, he could scarcely distinguish the transparent window from the opaque walls of his chamber. He was endeavouring to pierce the darkness with his ferret eyes, when the chimes of a neighbouring church struck the four quarters. So he listened for the hour.

To his great astonishment the heavy bell went on from six to seven, and from seven to eight, and regularly up to twelve; then stopped. Twelve! It was past two when he went to bed. The clock was wrong. An icicle must have got into the works. Twelve!

He touched the spring of his repeater, to correct this most preposterous clock. Its rapid little pulse beat twelve; and stopped.

"Why, it isn't possible," said Scrooge, "that I can have slept through a whole day and far into another night. It isn't possible that anything has happened to the sun, and this is twelve at noon!"

The idea being an alarming one, he scrambled out of bed,

and groped his way to the window. He was obliged to rub the frost off with the sleeve of his dressing-gown before he could see anything; and could see very little then. All he could make out was, that it was still very foggy and extremely cold, and that there was no noise of people running to and fro, and making a great stir, as there unquestionably would have been if night had beaten off bright day, and taken possession of the world. This was a great relief, because "Three days after sight of this First of Exchange pay to Mr. Ebenezer Scrooge or his order," and so forth, would have become a mere United States' security if there were no days to count by.

Scrooge went to bed again, and thought, and thought, and thought it over and over and over, and could make nothing of it. The more he thought, the more perplexed he was; and the more he endeavoured not to think, the more he thought.

Marley's Ghost bothered him exceedingly. Every time he resolved within himself, after mature inquiry, that it was all a dream, his mind flew back again, like a strong spring released, to its first position, and presented the same problem to be worked all through, "Was it a dream or not?"

Scrooge lay in this state until the chime had gone three quarters more, when he remembered, on a sudden, that the Ghost had warned him of a visitation when the bell tolled one. He resolved

to lie awake until the hour was passed; and, considering that he could no more go to sleep than go to Heaven, this was perhaps the wisest resolution in his power.

The quarter was so long, that he was more than once convinced he must have sunk into a doze unconsciously, and missed the clock. At length it broke upon his listening ear.

"Ding, dong!"

"A quarter past," said Scrooge, counting.

"Ding, dong!"

"Half-past!" said Scrooge.

"Ding, dong!"

"A quarter to it," said Scrooge.

"Ding, dong!"

"The hour itself," said Scrooge, triumphantly, "and nothing else!"

He spoke before the hour bell sounded, which it now did with a deep, dull, hollow, melancholy One. Light flashed up in the room upon the instant, and the curtains of his bed were drawn.

The curtains of his bed were drawn aside, I tell you, by a hand. Not the curtains at his feet, nor the curtains at his back, but those to which his face was addressed. The curtains of his bed were drawn aside; and Scrooge, starting up into a half-recumbent attitude, found himself face to face with the unearthly visitor who

drew them: as close to it as I am now to you, and I am standing in the spirit at your elbow.

It was a strange figure—like a child: yet not so like a child as like an old man, viewed through some supernatural medium, which gave him the appearance of having receded from the view, and being diminished to a child's proportions. Its hair, which hung about its neck and down its back, was white as if with age; and yet the face had not a wrinkle in it, and the tenderest bloom was on the skin. The arms were very long and muscular; the hands the same, as if its hold were of uncommon strength. Its legs and feet, most delicately formed, were, like those upper members, bare. It wore a tunic of the purest white; and round its waist was bound a lustrous belt, the sheen of which was beautiful. It held a branch of fresh green holly in its hand; and, in singular contradiction of that wintry emblem, had its dress trimmed with summer flowers. But the strangest thing about it was, that from the crown of its head there sprung a bright clear jet of light, by which all this was visible; and which was doubtless the occasion of its using, in its duller moments, a great extinguisher for a cap, which it now held under its arm.

Even this, though, when Scrooge looked at it with increasing steadiness, was *not* its strangest quality. For as its belt sparkled and glittered now in one part and now in another, and what

was light one instant, at another time was dark, so the figure itself fluctuated in its distinctness: being now a thing with one arm, now with one leg, now with twenty legs, now a pair of legs without a head, now a head without a body: of which dissolving parts, no outline would be visible in the dense gloom wherein they melted away. And in the very wonder of this, it would be itself again; distinct and clear as ever.

"Are you the Spirit, sir, whose coming was foretold to me?" asked Scrooge.

"I am!"

The voice was soft and gentle. Singularly low, as if instead of being so close beside him, it were at a distance.

"Who, and what are you?" Scrooge demanded.

"I am the Ghost of Christmas Past."

"Long Past?" inquired Scrooge: observant of its dwarfish stature.

"No. Your past."

Perhaps, Scrooge could not have told anybody why, if anybody could have asked him; but he had a special desire to see the Spirit in his cap; and begged him to be covered.

"What!" exclaimed the Ghost, "would you so soon put out, with worldly hands, the light I give? Is it not enough that you are one of those whose passions made this cap, and force me through

whole trains of years to wear it low upon my brow!"

Scrooge reverently disclaimed all intention to offend, or any knowledge of having wilfully "bonneted" the Spirit at any period of his life. He then made bold to inquire what business brought him there.

"Your welfare!" said the Ghost.

Scrooge expressed himself much obliged, but could not help thinking that a night of unbroken rest would have been more conducive to that end. The Spirit must have heard him thinking, for it said immediately:

"Your reclamation, then. Take heed!"

It put out its strong hand as it spoke, and clasped him gently by the arm.

"Rise! and walk with me!"

It would have been in vain for Scrooge to plead that the weather and the hour were not adapted to pedestrian purposes; that bed was warm, and the thermometer a long way below freezing; that he was clad but lightly in his slippers, dressing-gown, and nightcap; and that he had a cold upon him at that time. The grasp, though gentle as a woman's hand, was not to be resisted. He rose: but finding that the Spirit made towards the window, clasped his robe in supplication.

"I am a mortal," Scrooge remonstrated, "and liable to fall."

"Bear but a touch of my hand *there*," said the Spirit, laying it upon his heart, "and you shall be upheld in more than this!"

As the words were spoken, they passed through the wall, and stood upon an open country road, with fields on either hand. The city had entirely vanished. Not a vestige of it was to be seen. The darkness and the mist had vanished with it, for it was a clear, cold, winter day, with snow upon the ground.

"Good Heaven!" said Scrooge, clasping his hands together, as he looked about him. "I was bred in this place. I was a boy here!"

The Spirit gazed upon him mildly. Its gentle touch, though it had been light and instantaneous, appeared still present to the old man's sense of feeling. He was conscious of a thousand odours floating in the air, each one connected with a thousand thoughts, and hopes, and joys, and cares long, long, forgotten!

"Your lip is trembling," said the Ghost. "And what is that upon your cheek?"

Scrooge muttered, with an unusual catching in his voice, that it was a pimple; and begged the Ghost to lead him where he would.

"You recollect the way?" inquired the Spirit.

"Remember it!" cried Scrooge with fervour; "I could walk it blindfold."

"Strange to have forgotten it for so many years!" observed the Ghost. "Let us go on."

They walked along the road, Scrooge recognising every gate, and post, and tree; until a little market-town appeared in the distance, with its bridge, its church, and winding river. Some shaggy ponies now were seen trotting towards them with boys upon their backs, who called to other boys in country gigs and carts, driven by farmers. All these boys were in great spirits, and shouted to each other, until the broad fields were so full of merry music, that the crisp air laughed to hear it!

"These are but shadows of the things that have been," said the Ghost. "They have no consciousness of us."

The jocund travellers came on; and as they came, Scrooge knew and named them every one. Why was he rejoiced beyond all bounds to see them! Why did his cold eye glisten, and his heart leap up as they went past! Why was he filled with gladness when he heard them give each other Merry Christmas, as they parted at cross-roads and by-ways, for their several homes! What was merry Christmas to Scrooge? Out upon merry Christmas! What good had it ever done to him?

"The school is not quite deserted," said the Ghost. "A solitary child, neglected by his friends, is left there still."

Scrooge said he knew it. And he sobbed.

They left the high-road, by a well-remembered lane, and soon approached a mansion of dull red brick, with a little weathercock-

surmounted cupola, on the roof, and a bell hanging in it. It was a large house, but one of broken fortunes; for the spacious offices were little used, their walls were damp and mossy, their windows broken, and their gates decayed. Fowls clucked and strutted in the stables; and the coach-houses and sheds were over-run with grass. Nor was it more retentive of its ancient state, within; for entering the dreary hall, and glancing through the open doors of many rooms, they found them poorly furnished, cold, and vast. There was an earthy savour in the air, a chilly bareness in the place, which associated itself somehow with too much getting up by candle-light, and not too much to eat.

They went, the Ghost and Scrooge, across the hall, to a door at the back of the house. It opened before them, and disclosed a long, bare, melancholy room, made barer still by lines of plain deal forms and desks. At one of these a lonely boy was reading near a feeble fire; and Scrooge sat down upon a form, and wept to see his poor forgotten self as he had used to be.

Not a latent echo in the house, not a squeak and scuffle from the mice behind the panelling, not a drip from the half-thawed water-spout in the dull yard behind, not a sigh among the leafless boughs of one despondent poplar, not the idle swinging of an empty store-house door, no, not a clicking in the fire, but fell upon the heart of Scrooge with a softening influence, and gave a

freer passage to his tears.

The Spirit touched him on the arm, and pointed to his younger self, intent upon his reading. Suddenly a man, in foreign garments: wonderfully real and distinct to look at: stood outside the window, with an axe stuck in his belt, and leading by the bridle an ass laden with wood.

"Why, it's Ali Baba!" Scrooge exclaimed in ecstasy. "It's dear old honest Ali Baba! Yes, yes, I know! One Christmas time, when yonder solitary child was left here all alone, he did come, for the first time, just like that. Poor boy! And Valentine," said Scrooge, "and his wild brother, Orson; there they go! And what's his name, who was put down in his drawers, asleep, at the Gate of Damascus; don't you see him! And the Sultan's Groom turned upside down by the Genii; there he is upon his head! Serve him right. I'm glad of it. What business had *he* to be married to the Princess!"

To hear Scrooge expending all the earnestness of his nature on such subjects, in a most extraordinary voice between laughing and crying; and to see his heightened and excited face; would have been a surprise to his business friends in the city, indeed.

"There's the Parrot!" cried Scrooge. "Green body and yellow tail, with a thing like a lettuce growing out of the top of his head; there he is! Poor Robin Crusoe, he called him, when he came

home again after sailing round the island. 'Poor Robin Crusoe, where have you been, Robin Crusoe?' The man thought he was dreaming, but he wasn't. It was the Parrot, you know. There goes Friday, running for his life to the little creek! Halloa! Hoop! Halloo!"

Then, with a rapidity of transition very foreign to his usual character, he said, in pity for his former self, "Poor boy!" and cried again.

"I wish," Scrooge muttered, putting his hand in his pocket, and looking about him, after drying his eyes with his cuff: "but it's too late now."

"What is the matter?" asked the Spirit.

"Nothing," said Scrooge. "Nothing. There was a boy singing a Christmas Carol at my door last night. I should like to have given him something: that's all."

The Ghost smiled thoughtfully, and waved its hand: saying as it did so, "Let us see another Christmas!"

Scrooge's former self grew larger at the words, and the room became a little darker and more dirty. The panels shrunk, the windows cracked; fragments of plaster fell out of the ceiling, and the naked laths were shown instead; but how all this was brought about, Scrooge knew no more than you do. He only knew that it was quite correct; that everything had happened so; that there he

was, alone again, when all the other boys had gone home for the jolly holidays.

He was not reading now, but walking up and down despairingly. Scrooge looked at the Ghost, and with a mournful shaking of his head, glanced anxiously towards the door.

It opened; and a little girl, much younger than the boy, came darting in, and putting her arms about his neck, and often kissing him, addressed him as her "Dear, dear brother."

"I have come to bring you home, dear brother!" said the child, clapping her tiny hands, and bending down to laugh. "To bring you home, home, home!"

"Home, little Fan?" returned the boy.

"Yes!" said the child, brimful of glee. "Home, for good and all. Home, for ever and ever. Father is so much kinder than he used to be, that home's like Heaven! He spoke so gently to me one dear night when I was going to bed, that I was not afraid to ask him once more if you might come home; and he said Yes, you should; and sent me in a coach to bring you. And you're to be a man!" said the child, opening her eyes, "and are never to come back here; but first, we're to be together all the Christmas long, and have the merriest time in all the world."

"You are quite a woman, little Fan!" exclaimed the boy.

She clapped her hands and laughed, and tried to touch his head;

but being too little, laughed again, and stood on tiptoe to embrace him. Then she began to drag him, in her childish eagerness, towards the door; and he, nothing loth to go, accompanied her.

A terrible voice in the hall cried, "Bring down Master Scrooge's box, there!" and in the hall appeared the schoolmaster himself, who glared on Master Scrooge with a ferocious condescension, and threw him into a dreadful state of mind by shaking hands with him. He then conveyed him and his sister into the veriest old well of a shivering best-parlour that ever was seen, where the maps upon the wall, and the celestial and terrestrial globes in the windows, were waxy with cold. Here he produced a decanter of curiously light wine, and a block of curiously heavy cake, and administered instalments of those dainties to the young people: at the same time, sending out a meagre servant to offer a glass of "something" to the postboy, who answered that he thanked the gentleman, but if it was the same tap as he had tasted before, he had rather not. Master Scrooge's trunk being by this time tied on to the top of the chaise, the children bade the schoolmaster good-bye right willingly; and getting into it, drove gaily down the garden-sweep: the quick wheels dashing the hoar-frost and snow from off the dark leaves of the evergreens like spray.

"Always a delicate creature, whom a breath might have withered," said the Ghost. "But she had a large heart!"

"So she had," cried Scrooge. "You're right. I will not gainsay it, Spirit. God forbid!"

"She died a woman," said the Ghost, "and had, as I think, children."

"One child," Scrooge returned.

"True," said the Ghost. "Your nephew!"

Scrooge seemed uneasy in his mind; and answered briefly, "Yes."

Although they had but that moment left the school behind them, they were now in the busy thoroughfares of a city, where shadowy passengers passed and repassed; where shadowy carts and coaches battled for the way, and all the strife and tumult of a real city were. It was made plain enough, by the dressing of the shops, that here too it was Christmas time again; but it was evening, and the streets were lighted up.

The Ghost stopped at a certain warehouse door, and asked Scrooge if he knew it.

"Know it!" said Scrooge. "Was I apprenticed here!"

They went in. At sight of an old gentleman in a Welsh wig, sitting behind such a high desk, that if he had been two inches taller he must have knocked his head against the ceiling, Scrooge cried in great excitement:

"Why, it's old Fezziwig! Bless his heart; it's Fezziwig alive again!"

Old Fezziwig laid down his pen, and looked up at the clock, which pointed to the hour of seven. He rubbed his hands; adjusted his capacious waistcoat; laughed all over himself, from his shoes to his organ of benevolence; and called out in a comfortable, oily, rich, fat, jovial voice:

"Yo ho, there! Ebenezer! Dick!"

Scrooge's former self, now grown a young man, came briskly in, accompanied by his fellow-'prentice.

"Dick Wilkins, to be sure!" said Scrooge to the Ghost. "Bless me, yes. There he is. He was very much attached to me, was Dick. Poor Dick! Dear, dear!"

"Yo ho, my boys!" said Fezziwig. "No more work to-night. Christmas Eve, Dick. Christmas, Ebenezer! Let's have the shutters up," cried old Fezziwig, with a sharp clap of his hands, "before a man can say, Jack Robinson!"

You wouldn't believe how those two fellows went at it! They charged into the street with the shutters—one, two, three—had 'em up in their places—four, five, six—barred 'em and pinned 'em—seven, eight, nine—and came back before you could have got to twelve, panting like race-horses.

"Hilli-ho!" cried old Fezziwig, skipping down from the high desk, with wonderful agility. "Clear away, my lads, and let's have lots of room here! Hilli-ho, Dick! Chirrup, Ebenezer!"

Clear away! There was nothing they wouldn't have cleared away, or couldn't have cleared away, with old Fezziwig looking on. It was done in a minute. Every movable was packed off, as if it were dismissed from public life for evermore; the floor was swept and watered, the lamps were trimmed, fuel was heaped upon the fire; and the warehouse was as snug, and warm, and dry, and bright a ball-room, as you would desire to see upon a winter's night.

In came a fiddler with a music-book, and went up to the lofty desk, and made an orchestra of it, and tuned like fifty stomach-aches. In came Mrs. Fezziwig, one vast substantial smile. In came the three Miss Fezziwigs, beaming and lovable. In came the six young followers whose hearts they broke. In came all the young men and women employed in the business. In came the housemaid, with her cousin, the baker. In came the cook, with her brother's particular friend, the milkman. In came the boy from over the way, who was suspected of not having board enough from his master; trying to hide himself behind the girl from next door but one, who was proved to have had her ears pulled by her Mistress. In they all came, one after another; some shyly, some boldly, some gracefully, some awkwardly, some pushing, some pulling; in they all came, anyhow and everyhow. Away they all went, twenty couple at once; hands half round and back again

the other way; down the middle and up again; round and round in various stages of affectionate grouping; old top couple always turning up in the wrong place; new top couple starting off again, as soon as they got there; all top couples at last, and not a bottom one to help them! When this result was brought about, old Fezziwig, clapping his hands to stop the dance, cried out, "Well done!" and the fiddler plunged his hot face into a pot of porter, especially provided for that purpose. But scorning rest, upon his reappearance, he instantly began again, though there were no dancers yet, as if the other fiddler had been carried home, exhausted, on a shutter, and he were a bran-new man resolved to beat him out of sight, or perish.

There were more dances, and there were forfeits, and more dances, and there was cake, and there was negus, and there was a great piece of Cold Roast, and there was a great piece of Cold Boiled, and there were mince-pies, and plenty of beer. But the great effect of the evening came after the Roast and Boiled, when the fiddler (an artful dog, mind! The sort of man who knew his business better than you or I could have told it him!) struck up "Sir Roger de Coverley." Then old Fezziwig stood out to dance with Mrs. Fezziwig. Top couple, too; with a good stiff piece of work cut out for them; three or four and twenty pair of partners; people who were not to be trifled with; people who *would* dance,

and had no notion of walking.

But if they had been twice as many—ah, four times—old Fezziwig would have been a match for them, and so would Mrs. Fezziwig. As to *her*, she was worthy to be his partner in every sense of the term. If that's not high praise, tell me higher, and I'll use it. A positive light appeared to issue from Fezziwig's calves. They shone in every part of the dance like moons. You couldn't have predicted, at any given time, what would have become of them next. And when old Fezziwig and Mrs. Fezziwig had gone all through the dance; advance and retire, both hands to your partner, bow and curtsey, corkscrew, thread-the-needle, and back again to your place; Fezziwig "cut"—cut so deftly, that he appeared to wink with his legs, and came upon his feet again without a stagger.

When the clock struck eleven, this domestic ball broke up. Mr. and Mrs. Fezziwig took their stations, one on either side of the door, and shaking hands with every person individually as he or she went out, wished him or her a Merry Christmas. When everybody had retired but the two 'prentices, they did the same to them; and thus the cheerful voices died away, and the lads were left to their beds; which were under a counter in the back-shop.

During the whole of this time, Scrooge had acted like a man out of his wits. His heart and soul were in the scene, and with his

former self. He corroborated everything, remembered everything, enjoyed everything, and underwent the strangest agitation. It was not until now, when the bright faces of his former self and Dick were turned from them, that he remembered the Ghost, and became conscious that it was looking full upon him, while the light upon its head burnt very clear.

"A small matter," said the Ghost, "to make these silly folks so full of gratitude."

"Small!" echoed Scrooge.

The Spirit signed to him to listen to the two apprentices, who were pouring out their hearts in praise of Fezziwig: and when he had done so, said,

"Why! Is it not? He has spent but a few pounds of your mortal money: three or four perhaps. Is that so much that he deserves this praise?"

"It isn't that," said Scrooge, heated by the remark, and speaking unconsciously like his former, not his latter, self. "It isn't that, Spirit. He has the power to render us happy or unhappy; to make our service light or burdensome; a pleasure or a toil. Say that his power lies in words and looks; in things so slight and insignificant that it is impossible to add and count 'em up: what then? The happiness he gives, is quite as great as if it cost a fortune."

He felt the Spirit's glance, and stopped.

"What is the matter?" asked the Ghost.

"Nothing particular," said Scrooge.

"Something, I think?" the Ghost insisted.

"No," said Scrooge, "No. I should like to be able to say a word or two to my clerk just now. That's all."

His former self turned down the lamps as he gave utterance to the wish; and Scrooge and the Ghost again stood side by side in the open air.

"My time grows short," observed the Spirit. "Quick!"

This was not addressed to Scrooge, or to any one whom he could see, but it produced an immediate effect. For again Scrooge saw himself. He was older now; a man in the prime of life. His face had not the harsh and rigid lines of later years; but it had begun to wear the signs of care and avarice. There was an eager, greedy, restless motion in the eye, which showed the passion that had taken root, and where the shadow of the growing tree would fall.

He was not alone, but sat by the side of a fair young girl in a mourning-dress: in whose eyes there were tears, which sparkled in the light that shone out of the Ghost of Christmas Past.

"It matters little," she said, softly. "To you, very little. Another idol has displaced me; and if it can cheer and comfort you in time to come, as I would have tried to do, I have no just cause to

grieve."

"What Idol has displaced you?" he rejoined.

"A golden one."

"This is the even-handed dealing of the world!" he said. "There is nothing on which it is so hard as poverty; and there is nothing it professes to condemn with such severity as the pursuit of wealth!"

"You fear the world too much," she answered, gently. "All your other hopes have merged into the hope of being beyond the chance of its sordid reproach. I have seen your nobler aspirations fall off one by one, until the master-passion, Gain, engrosses you. Have I not?"

"What then?" he retorted. "Even if I have grown so much wiser, what then? I am not changed towards you."

She shook her head.

"Am I?"

"Our contract is an old one. It was made when we were both poor and content to be so, until, in good season, we could improve our worldly fortune by our patient industry. You are changed. When it was made, you were another man."

"I was a boy," he said impatiently.

"Your own feeling tells you that you were not what you are," she returned. "I am. That which promised happiness when we

were one in heart, is fraught with misery now that we are two. How often and how keenly I have thought of this, I will not say. It is enough that I have thought of it, and can release you."

"Have I ever sought release?"

"In words. No. Never."

"In what, then?"

"In a changed nature; in an altered spirit; in another atmosphere of life; another Hope as its great end. In everything that made my love of any worth or value in your sight. If this had never been between us," said the girl, looking mildly, but with steadiness, upon him; "tell me, would you seek me out and try to win me now? Ah, no!"

He seemed to yield to the justice of this supposition, in spite of himself. But he said with a struggle, "You think not."

"I would gladly think otherwise if I could," she answered, "Heaven knows! When I have learned a Truth like this, I know how strong and irresistible it must be. But if you were free to-day, to-morrow, yesterday, can even I believe that you would choose a dowerless girl—you who, in your very confidence with her, weigh everything by Gain: or, choosing her, if for a moment you were false enough to your one guiding principle to do so, do I not know that your repentance and regret would surely follow? I do; and I release you. With a full heart, for the love of him you once

were."

He was about to speak; but with her head turned from him, she resumed.

"You may—the memory of what is past half makes me hope you will—have pain in this. A very, very brief time, and you will dismiss the recollection of it, gladly, as an unprofitable dream, from which it happened well that you awoke. May you be happy in the life you have chosen!"

She left him, and they parted.

"Spirit!" said Scrooge, "show me no more! Conduct me home. Why do you delight to torture me?"

"One shadow more!" exclaimed the Ghost.

"No more!" cried Scrooge. "No more. I don't wish to see it. Show me no more!"

But the relentless Ghost pinioned him in both his arms, and forced him to observe what happened next.

They were in another scene and place; a room, not very large or handsome, but full of comfort. Near to the winter fire sat a beautiful young girl, so like that last that Scrooge believed it was the same, until he saw her, now a comely matron, sitting opposite her daughter. The noise in this room was perfectly tumultuous, for there were more children there, than Scrooge in his agitated state of mind could count; and, unlike the celebrated herd in

the poem, they were not forty children conducting themselves like one, but every child was conducting itself like forty. The consequences were uproarious beyond belief; but no one seemed to care; on the contrary, the mother and daughter laughed heartily, and enjoyed it very much; and the latter, soon beginning to mingle in the sports, got pillaged by the young brigands most ruthlessly. What would I not have given to be one of them! Though I never could have been so rude, no, no! I wouldn't for the wealth of all the world have crushed that braided hair, and torn it down; and for the precious little shoe, I wouldn't have plucked it off, God bless my soul! to save my life. As to measuring her waist in sport, as they did, bold young brood, I couldn't have done it; I should have expected my arm to have grown round it for a punishment, and never come straight again. And yet I should have dearly liked, I own, to have touched her lips; to have questioned her, that she might have opened them; to have looked upon the lashes of her downcast eyes, and never raised a blush; to have let loose waves of hair, an inch of which would be a keepsake beyond price: in short, I should have liked, I do confess, to have had the lightest licence of a child, and yet to have been man enough to know its value.

But now a knocking at the door was heard, and such a rush immediately ensued that she with laughing face and plundered

dress was borne towards it the centre of a flushed and boisterous group, just in time to greet the father, who came home attended by a man laden with Christmas toys and presents. Then the shouting and the struggling, and the onslaught that was made on the defenceless porter! The scaling him with chairs for ladders to dive into his pockets, despoil him of brown-paper parcels, hold on tight by his cravat, hug him round his neck, pommel his back, and kick his legs in irrepressible affection! The shouts of wonder and delight with which the development of every package was received! The terrible announcement that the baby had been taken in the act of putting a doll's frying-pan into his mouth, and was more than suspected of having swallowed a fictitious turkey, glued on a wooden platter! The immense relief of finding this a false alarm! The joy, and gratitude, and ecstasy! They are all indescribable alike. It is enough that by degrees the children and their emotions got out of the parlour, and by one stair at a time, up to the top of the house; where they went to bed, and so subsided.

And now Scrooge looked on more attentively than ever, when the master of the house, having his daughter leaning fondly on him, sat down with her and her mother at his own fireside; and when he thought that such another creature, quite as graceful and as full of promise, might have called him father, and been a

spring-time in the haggard winter of his life, his sight grew very dim indeed.

"Belle," said the husband, turning to his wife with a smile, "I saw an old friend of yours this afternoon."

"Who was it?"

"Guess!"

"How can I? Tut, don't I know?" she added in the same breath, laughing as he laughed. "Mr. Scrooge."

"Mr. Scrooge it was. I passed his office window; and as it was not shut up, and he had a candle inside, I could scarcely help seeing him. His partner lies upon the point of death, I hear; and there he sat alone. Quite alone in the world, I do believe."

"Spirit!" said Scrooge in a broken voice, "remove me from this place."

"I told you these were shadows of the things that have been," said the Ghost. "That they are what they are, do not blame me!"

"Remove me!" Scrooge exclaimed, "I cannot bear it!"

He turned upon the Ghost, and seeing that it looked upon him with a face, in which in some strange way there were fragments of all the faces it had shown him, wrestled with it.

"Leave me! Take me back. Haunt me no longer!"

In the struggle, if that can be called a struggle in which the Ghost with no visible resistance on its own part was undisturbed

by any effort of its adversary, Scrooge observed that its light was burning high and bright; and dimly connecting that with its influence over him, he seized the extinguisher-cap, and by a sudden action pressed it down upon its head.

The Spirit dropped beneath it, so that the extinguisher covered its whole form; but though Scrooge pressed it down with all his force, he could not hide the light, which streamed from under it, in an unbroken flood upon the ground.

He was conscious of being exhausted, and overcome by an irresistible drowsiness; and, further, of being in his own bed-room. He gave the cap a parting squeeze, in which his hand relaxed; and had barely time to reel to bed, before he sank into a heavy sleep.

STAVE III

THE SECOND OF THE THREE SPIRITS

Awaking in the middle of a prodigiously tough snore, and sitting up in bed to get his thoughts together, Scrooge had no occasion to be told that the bell was again upon the stroke of One. He felt that he was restored to consciousness in the right nick of time, for the especial purpose of holding a conference with the second messenger dispatched to him through Jacob Marley's intervention. But finding that he turned uncomfortably cold when he began to wonder which of his curtains this new spectre would draw back, he put them every one aside with his own hands, and lying down again, established a sharp look-out all round the bed. For he wished to challenge the Spirit on the moment of its appearance, and did not wish to be taken by surprise, and made nervous.

Gentlemen of the free-and-easy sort, who plume themselves on being acquainted with a move or two, and being usually equal to the time-of-day, express the wide range of their capacity for adventure by observing that they are good for anything

from pitch-and-toss to manslaughter; between which opposite extremes, no doubt, there lies a tolerably wide and comprehensive range of subjects. Without venturing for Scrooge quite as hardily as this, I don't mind calling on you to believe that he was ready for a good broad field of strange appearances, and that nothing between a baby and rhinoceros would have astonished him very much.

Now, being prepared for almost anything, he was not by any means prepared for nothing; and, consequently, when the Bell struck One, and no shape appeared, he was taken with a violent fit of trembling. Five minutes, ten minutes, a quarter of an hour went by, yet nothing came. All this time, he lay upon his bed, the very core and centre of a blaze of ruddy light, which streamed upon it when the clock proclaimed the hour; and which, being only light, was more alarming than a dozen ghosts, as he was powerless to make out what it meant, or would be at; and was sometimes apprehensive that he might be at that very moment an interesting case of spontaneous combustion, without having the consolation of knowing it. At last, however, he began to think— as you or I would have thought at first; for it is always the person not in the predicament who knows what ought to have been done in it, and would unquestionably have done it too—at last, I say, he began to think that the source and secret of this ghostly light might be in the adjoining room, from whence, on further tracing

it, it seemed to shine. This idea taking full possession of his mind, he got up softly and shuffled in his slippers to the door.

The moment Scrooge's hand was on the lock, a strange voice called him by his name, and bade him enter. He obeyed.

It was his own room. There was no doubt about that. But it had undergone a surprising transformation. The walls and ceiling were so hung with living green, that it looked a perfect grove; from every part of which, bright gleaming berries glistened. The crisp leaves of holly, mistletoe, and ivy reflected back the light, as if so many little mirrors had been scattered there; and such a mighty blaze went roaring up the chimney, as that dull petrifaction of a hearth had never known in Scrooge's time, or Marley's, or for many and many a winter season gone. Heaped up on the floor, to form a kind of throne, were turkeys, geese, game, poultry, brawn, great joints of meat, sucking-pigs, long wreaths of sausages, mince-pies, plum-puddings, barrels of oysters, red-hot chestnuts, cherry-cheeked apples, juicy oranges, luscious pears, immense twelfth-cakes, and seething bowls of punch, that made the chamber dim with their delicious steam. In easy state upon this couch, there sat a jolly Giant, glorious to see: who bore a glowing torch, in shape not unlike Plenty's horn, and held it up, high up, to shed its light on Scrooge, as he came peeping round the door.

"Come in!" exclaimed the Ghost. "Come in, and know me

better, man!"

Scrooge entered timidly, and hung his head before this Spirit. He was not the dogged Scrooge he had been; and though the Spirit's eyes were clear and kind, he did not like to meet them.

"I am the Ghost of Christmas Present," said the Spirit. "Look upon me!"

Scrooge reverently did so. It was clothed in one simple green robe, or mantle, bordered with white fur. This garment hung so loosely on the figure, that its capacious breast was bare, as if disdaining to be warded or concealed by any artifice. Its feet, observable beneath the ample folds of the garment, were also bare; and on its head it wore no other covering than a holly wreath, set here and there with shining icicles. Its dark brown curls were long and free; free as its genial face, its sparkling eye, its open hand, its cheery voice, its unconstrained demeanour, and its joyful air. Girded round its middle was an antique scabbard; but no sword was in it, and the ancient sheath was eaten up with rust.

"You have never seen the like of me before!" exclaimed the Spirit.

"Never," Scrooge made answer to it.

"Have never walked forth with the younger members of my family; meaning (for I am very young) my elder brothers born in these later years?" pursued the Phantom.

"I don't think I have," said Scrooge. "I am afraid I have not. Have you had many brothers, Spirit?"

"More than eighteen hundred," said the Ghost.

"A tremendous family to provide for!" muttered Scrooge.

The Ghost of Christmas Present rose.

"Spirit," said Scrooge submissively, "conduct me where you will. I went forth last night on compulsion, and I learnt a lesson which is working now. To-night, if you have aught to teach me, let me profit by it."

"Touch my robe!"

Scrooge did as he was told, and held it fast.

Holly, mistletoe, red berries, ivy, turkeys, geese, game, poultry, brawn, meat, pigs, sausages, oysters, pies, puddings, fruit, and punch, all vanished instantly. So did the room, the fire, the ruddy glow, the hour of night, and they stood in the city streets on Christmas morning, where (for the weather was severe) the people made a rough, but brisk and not unpleasant kind of music, in scraping the snow from the pavement in front of their dwellings, and from the tops of their houses, whence it was mad delight to the boys to see it come plumping down into the road below, and splitting into artificial little snow-storms.

The house fronts looked black enough, and the windows blacker, contrasting with the smooth white sheet of snow upon the roofs, and with the dirtier snow upon the ground; which

last deposit had been ploughed up in deep furrows by the heavy wheels of carts and waggons; furrows that crossed and re-crossed each other hundreds of times where the great streets branched off; and made intricate channels, hard to trace in the thick yellow mud and icy water. The sky was gloomy, and the shortest streets were choked up with a dingy mist, half thawed, half frozen, whose heavier particles descended in a shower of sooty atoms, as if all the chimneys in Great Britain had, by one consent, caught fire, and were blazing away to their dear hearts' content. There was nothing very cheerful in the climate or the town, and yet was there an air of cheerfulness abroad that the clearest summer air and brightest summer sun might have endeavoured to diffuse in vain.

For the people who were shovelling away on the housetops were jovial and full of glee; calling out to one another from the parapets, and now and then exchanging a facetious snowball— better-natured missile far than many a wordy jest—laughing heartily if it went right and not less heartily if it went wrong. The poulterers' shops were still half open, and the fruiterers' were radiant in their glory. There were great, round, pot-bellied baskets of chestnuts, shaped like the waistcoats of jolly old gentlemen, lolling at the doors, and tumbling out into the street in their apoplectic opulence. There were ruddy, brown-faced, broad-girthed Spanish Onions, shining in the fatness of their

growth like Spanish Friars, and winking from their shelves in wanton slyness at the girls as they went by, and glanced demurely at the hung-up mistletoe. There were pears and apples, clustered high in blooming pyramids; there were bunches of grapes, made, in the shopkeepers benevolence to dangle from conspicuous hooks, that people's mouths might water gratis as they passed; there were piles of filberts, mossy and brown, recalling, in their fragrance, ancient walks among the woods, and pleasant shufflings ankle deep through withered leaves; there were Norfolk Biffins, squat and swarthy, setting off the yellow of the oranges and lemons, and, in the great compactness of their juicy persons, urgently entreating and beseeching to be carried home in paper bags and eaten after dinner. The very gold and silver fish, set forth among these choice fruits in a bowl, though members of a dull and stagnant-blooded race, appeared to know that there was something going on; and, to a fish, went gasping round and round their little world in slow and passionless excitement.

The Grocers'! oh, the Grocers'! nearly closed, with perhaps two shutters down, or one; but through those gaps such glimpses! It was not alone that the scales descending on the counter made a merry sound, or that the twine and roller parted company so briskly, or that the canisters were rattled up and down like juggling tricks, or even that the blended scents of tea and coffee were so grateful to the nose, or even that the raisins were so

plentiful and rare, the almonds so extremely white, the sticks of cinnamon so long and straight, the other spices so delicious, the candied fruits so caked and spotted with molten sugar as to make the coldest lookers-on feel faint and subsequently bilious. Nor was it that the figs were moist and pulpy, or that the French plums blushed in modest tartness from their highly-decorated boxes, or that everything was good to eat and in its Christmas dress; but the customers were all so hurried and so eager in the hopeful promise of the day, that they tumbled up against each other at the door, crashing their wicker baskets wildly, and left their purchases upon the counter, and came running back to fetch them, and committed hundreds of the like mistakes, in the best humour possible; while the Grocer and his people were so frank and fresh that the polished hearts with which they fastened their aprons behind might have been their own, worn outside for general inspection, and for Christmas daws to peck at if they chose.

But soon the steeples called good people all, to church and chapel, and away they came, flocking through the streets in their best clothes, and with their gayest faces. And at the same time there emerged from scores of bye-streets, lanes, and nameless turnings, innumerable people, carrying their dinners to the bakers' shops. The sight of these poor revellers appeared to interest the Spirit very much, for he stood with Scrooge beside

him in a baker's doorway, and taking off the covers as their bearers passed, sprinkled incense on their dinners from his torch. And it was a very uncommon kind of torch, for once or twice when there were angry words between some dinner-carriers who had jostled each other, he shed a few drops of water on them from it, and their good humour was restored directly. For they said, it was a shame to quarrel upon Christmas Day. And so it was! God love it, so it was!

In time the bells ceased, and the bakers were shut up; and yet there was a genial shadowing forth of all these dinners and the progress of their cooking, in the thawed blotch of wet above each baker's oven; where the pavement smoked as if its stones were cooking too.

"Is there a peculiar flavour in what you sprinkle from your torch?" asked Scrooge.

"There is. My own."

"Would it apply to any kind of dinner on this day?" asked Scrooge.

"To any kindly given. To a poor one most."

"Why to a poor one most?" asked Scrooge.

"Because it needs it most."

"Spirit," said Scrooge, after a moment's thought, "I wonder you, of all the beings in the many worlds about us, should desire to cramp these people's opportunities of innocent enjoyment."

"I!" cried the Spirit.

"You would deprive them of their means of dining every seventh day, often the only day on which they can be said to dine at all," said Scrooge. "Wouldn't you?"

"I!" cried the Spirit.

"You seek to close these places on the Seventh Day?" said Scrooge. "And it comes to the same thing."

"*I* seek!" exclaimed the Spirit.

"Forgive me if I am wrong. It has been done in your name, or at least in that of your family," said Scrooge.

"There are some upon this earth of yours," returned the Spirit, "who lay claim to know us, and who do their deeds of passion, pride, ill-will, hatred, envy, bigotry, and selfishness in our name, who are as strange to us and all our kith and kin, as if they had never lived. Remember that, and charge their doings on themselves, not us."

Scrooge promised that he would; and they went on, invisible, as they had been before, into the suburbs of the town. It was a remarkable quality of the Ghost (which Scrooge had observed at the baker's), that notwithstanding his gigantic size, he could accommodate himself to any place with ease; and that he stood beneath a low roof quite as gracefully and like a supernatural creature, as it was possible he could have done in any lofty hall.

And perhaps it was the pleasure the good Spirit had in showing

off this power of his, or else it was his own kind, generous, hearty nature, and his sympathy with all poor men, that led him straight to Scrooge's clerk's; for there he went, and took Scrooge with him, holding to his robe; and on the threshold of the door the Spirit smiled, and stopped to bless Bob Cratchit's dwelling with the sprinkling of his torch. Think of that! Bob had but fifteen "Bob" a-week himself; he pocketed on Saturdays but fifteen copies of his Christian name; and yet the Ghost of Christmas Present blessed his four-roomed house!

Then up rose Mrs. Cratchit, Cratchit's wife, dressed out but poorly in a twice-turned gown, but brave in ribbons, which are cheap and make a goodly show for sixpence; and she laid the cloth, assisted by Belinda Cratchit, second of her daughters, also brave in ribbons; while Master Peter Cratchit plunged a fork into the saucepan of potatoes, and getting the corners of his monstrous shirt collar (Bob's private property, conferred upon his son and heir in honour of the day) into his mouth, rejoiced to find himself so gallantly attired, and yearned to show his linen in the fashionable Parks. And now two smaller Cratchits, boy and girl, came tearing in, screaming that outside the baker's they had smelt the goose, and known it for their own; and basking in luxurious thoughts of sage and onion, these young Cratchits danced about the table, and exalted Master Peter Cratchit to the skies, while he (not proud, although his collars nearly choked him) blew the

fire, until the slow potatoes bubbling up, knocked loudly at the saucepan-lid to be let out and peeled.

"What has ever got your precious father then?" said Mrs. Cratchit. "And your brother, Tiny Tim! And Martha warn't as late last Christmas Day by half-an-hour?"

"Here's Martha, mother!" said a girl, appearing as she spoke.

"Here's Martha, mother!" cried the two young Cratchits. "Hurrah! There's such a goose, Martha!"

"Why, bless your heart alive, my dear, how late you are!" said Mrs. Cratchit, kissing her a dozen times, and taking off her shawl and bonnet for her with officious zeal.

"We'd a deal of work to finish up last night," replied the girl, "and had to clear away this morning, mother!"

"Well! Never mind so long as you are come," said Mrs. Cratchit. "Sit ye down before the fire, my dear, and have a warm, Lord bless ye!"

"No, no! There's father coming," cried the two young Cratchits, who were everywhere at once. "Hide, Martha, hide!"

So Martha hid herself, and in came little Bob, the father, with at least three feet of comforter exclusive of the fringe, hanging down before him; and his thread-bare clothes darned up and brushed, to look seasonable; and Tiny Tim upon his shoulder. Alas for Tiny Tim, he bore a little crutch, and had his limbs supported by an iron frame!

"Why, where's our Martha?" cried Bob Cratchit, looking round.

"Not coming," said Mrs. Cratchit.

"Not coming!" said Bob, with a sudden declension in his high spirits; for he had been Tim's blood horse all the way from church, and had come home rampant. "Not coming upon Christmas Day!"

Martha didn't like to see him disappointed, if it were only in joke; so she came out prematurely from behind the closet door, and ran into his arms, while the two young Cratchits hustled Tiny Tim, and bore him off into the wash-house, that he might hear the pudding singing in the copper. "And how did little Tim behave?" asked Mrs. Cratchit, when she had rallied Bob on his credulity, and Bob had hugged his daughter to his heart's content. "As good as gold," said Bob, "and better. Somehow he gets thoughtful, sitting by himself so much, and thinks the strangest things you ever heard. He told me, coming home, that he hoped the people saw him in the church, because he was a cripple, and it might be pleasant to them to remember upon Christmas Day, who made lame beggars walk, and blind men see." Bob's voice was tremulous when he told them this, and trembled more when he said that Tiny Tim was growing strong and hearty.

His active little crutch was heard upon the floor, and back

came Tiny Tim before another word was spoken, escorted by his brother and sister to his stool before the fire; and while Bob, turning up his cuffs—as if, poor fellow, they were capable of being made more shabby—compounded some hot mixture in a jug with gin and lemons, and stirred it round and round and put it on the hob to simmer; Master Peter, and the two ubiquitous young Cratchits went to fetch the goose, with which they soon returned in high procession.

Such a bustle ensued that you might have thought a goose the rarest of all birds; a feathered phenomenon, to which a black swan was a matter of course—and in truth it was something very like it in that house. Mrs. Cratchit made the gravy (ready beforehand in a little saucepan) hissing hot; Master Peter mashed the potatoes with incredible vigour; Miss Belinda sweetened up the apple-sauce; Martha dusted the hot plates; Bob took Tiny Tim beside him in a tiny corner at the table; the two young Cratchits set chairs for everybody, not forgetting themselves, and mounting guard upon their posts, crammed spoons into their mouths, lest they should shriek for goose before their turn came to be helped. At last the dishes were set on, and grace was said. It was succeeded by a breathless pause, as Mrs. Cratchit, looking slowly all along the carving-knife, prepared to plunge it in the breast; but when she did, and when the long expected gush of stuffing issued forth, one murmur of delight arose all round the board, and even Tiny

Tim, excited by the two young Cratchits, beat on the table with the handle of his knife, and feebly cried Hurrah!

There never was such a goose. Bob said he didn't believe there ever was such a goose cooked. Its tenderness and flavour, size and cheapness, were the themes of universal admiration. Eked out by apple-sauce and mashed potatoes, it was a sufficient dinner for the whole family; indeed, as Mrs. Cratchit said with great delight (surveying one small atom of abone upon the dish), they hadn't ate it all at last! Yet every one had had enough, and the youngest Cratchits in particular, were steeped in sage and onion to the eyebrows! But now, the plates being changed by Miss Belinda, Mrs. Cratchit left the room alone—too nervous tobear witnesses—to take the pudding up and bring it in.

Suppose it should not be done enough! Suppose it should break in turning out! Suppose somebody should have got over the wall of the back-yard, and stolen it, while they weremerry with the goose—a supposition at which the two young Cratchits became livid! All sorts of horrors were supposed.

Hallo! A great deal of steam! The pudding was out of the copper. A smell like a washing-day! That was the cloth. A smell like an eating-house and a pastrycook's next door to each other, with a laundress's next door to that! That was the pudding! In half a minute Mrs. Cratchit entered—flushed, but smiling proudly— with the pudding, like a speckled cannon-ball, so hard and firm,

blazing in half of half-a-quartern of ignited brandy, and bedight with Christmas holly stuck into the top.

Oh, a wonderful pudding! Bob Cratchit said, and calmly too, that he regarded it as the greatest success achieved by Mrs. Cratchit since their marriage. Mrs. Cratchit said that now the weight was off her mind, she would confess she had had her doubts about the quantity of flour. Everybody had something to say about it, but nobody said or thought it was at all asmall pudding for a large family. It would have been flat heresy to do so. Any Cratchit would have blushed to hint at such a thing.

At last the dinner was all done, the cloth was cleared, the hearth swept, and the fire made up. The compound in the jug being tasted, and considered perfect, apples and oranges were put upon the table, and a shovel-full of chestnuts on the fire. Then all the Cratchit family drew round the hearth, in what Bob Cratchit called a circle, meaning half a one; and at Bob Cratchit's elbow stood the family display of glass. Two tumblers, and a custard-cup without a handle.

These held the hot stuff from the jug, however, as well as golden goblets would have done; and Bob served it out with beaming looks, while the chestnuts on the fire sputtered and cracked noisily. Then Bob proposed: "A Merry Christmas to us all, my dears. God bless us!" Which all the family re-echoed.

"God bless us every one!" said Tiny Tim, the last of all. He sat

very close to his father's side upon his little stool. Bob held his withered little hand in his, as if he loved the child, and wished to keep him by his side, and dreaded that he might be taken from him.

"Spirit," said Scrooge, with an interest he had never felt before, "tell me if Tiny Tim will live."

"I see a vacant seat," replied the Ghost, "in the poor chimney-corner, and a crutch without an owner, carefully preserved. If these shadows remain unaltered by the Future, the child will die."

"No, no," said Scrooge. "Oh, no, kind Spirit! say he will be spared."

"If these shadows remain unaltered by the Future, none other of my race," returned the Ghost, "will find him here. What then? If he be like to die, he had better do it, and decrease the surplus population."

Scrooge hung his head to hear his own words quoted by the Spirit, and was overcome with penitence and grief.

"Man," said the Ghost, "if man you be in heart, not adamant, forbear that wicked cant until you have discovered What the surplus is, and Where it is. Will you decide what men shall live, what men shall die? It may be, that in the sight of Heaven, you are more worthless and less fit to live than millions like this poor man's child. Oh God! to hear the Insect on the leaf pronouncing on the too much life among his hungry brothers in the dust!"

Scrooge bent before the Ghost's rebuke, and trembling cast his eyes upon the ground. But he raised them speedily, on hearing his own name.

"Mr. Scrooge!" said Bob; "I'll give you Mr. Scrooge, the Founder of the Feast!"

"The Founder of the Feast indeed!" cried Mrs. Cratchit, reddening. "I wish I had him here. I'd give him a piece of my mind to feast upon, and I hope he'd have a good appetite for it."

"My dear," said Bob, "the children! Christmas Day."

"It should be Christmas Day, I am sure," said she, "on which one drinks the health of such an odious, stingy, hard, unfeeling man as Mr. Scrooge. You know he is, Robert! Nobody knows it better than you do, poor fellow!"

"My dear," was Bob's mild answer, "Christmas Day."

"I'll drink his health for your sake and the Day's," said Mrs. Cratchit, "not for his. Long life to him! A merry Christmas and a happy new year! He'll be very merry and very happy, I have no doubt!"

The children drank the toast after her. It was the first of their proceedings which had no heartiness. Tiny Tim drank it last of all, but he didn't care twopence for it. Scrooge was the Ogre of the family. The mention of his name cast a dark shadow on the party, which was not dispelled for full five minutes.

After it had passed away, they were ten times merrier than

before, from the mere relief of Scrooge the Baleful being done with. Bob Cratchit told them how he had a situation in his eye for Master Peter, which would bring in, if obtained, full five-and-sixpence weekly. The two young Cratchits laughed tremendously at the idea of Peter's being a man of business; and Peter himself looked thoughtfully at the fire from between his collars, as if he were deliberating what particular investments he should favour when he came into the receipt of that bewildering income. Martha, who was a poor apprentice at a milliner's, then told them what kind of work she had to do, and how many hours she worked at a stretch, and how she meant to lie abed to-morrow morning for a good long rest; to-morrow being a holiday she passed at home. Also how she had seen a countess and a lord some days before, and how the lord "was much about as tall as Peter;" at which Peter pulled up his collars so high that you couldn't have seen his head if you had been there. All this time the chestnuts and the jug went round and round; and by-and-bye they had a song, about a lost child travelling in the snow, from Tiny Tim, who had a plaintive little voice, and sang it very well indeed.

There was nothing of high mark in this. They were not a handsome family; they were not well dressed; their shoes were far from being water-proof; their clothes were scanty; and Peter might have known, and very likely did, the inside of a pawnbroker's. But, they were happy, grateful, pleased with one

another, and contented with the time; and when they faded, and looked happier yet in the bright sprinklings of the Spirit's torch at parting, Scrooge had his eye upon them, and especially on Tiny Tim, until the last.

By this time it was getting dark, and snowing pretty heavily; and as Scrooge and the Spirit went along the streets, the brightness of the roaring fires in kitchens, parlours, and all sorts of rooms, was wonderful. Here, the flickering of the blaze showed preparations for a cosy dinner, with hot plates baking through and through before the fire, and deep red curtains, ready to be drawn to shut out cold and darkness. There all the children of the house were running out into the snow to meet their married sisters, brothers, cousins, uncles, aunts, and be the first to greet them. Here, again, were shadows on the window-blind of guests assembling; and there a group of handsome girls, all hooded and fur-booted, and all chattering at once, tripped lightly off to some near neighbour's house; where, woe upon the single man who saw them enter—artful witches, well they knew it—in a glow!

But, if you had judged from the numbers of people on their way to friendly gatherings, you might have thought that no one was at home to give them welcome when they got there, instead of every house expecting company, and piling up its fires half-chimney high. Blessings on it, how the Ghost exulted! How it bared its breadth of breast, and opened its capacious palm, and floated on,

outpouring, with a generous hand, its bright and harmless mirth on everything within its reach! The very lamplighter, who ran on before, dotting the dusky street with specks of light, and who was dressed to spend the evening somewhere, laughed out loudly as the Spirit passed, though little kenned the lamplighter that he had any company but Christmas!

And now, without a word of warning from the Ghost, they stood upon a bleak and desert moor, where monstrous masses of rude stone were cast about, as though it were the burial-place of giants; and water spread itself wheresoever it listed, or would have done so, but for the frost that held it prisoner; and nothing grew but moss and furze, and coarse rank grass. Down in the west the setting sun had left a streak of fiery red, which glared upon the desolation for an instant, like a sullen eye, and frowning lower, lower, lower yet, was lost in the thick gloom of darkest night.

"What place is this?" asked Scrooge.

"A place where Miners live, who labour in the bowels of the earth," returned the Spirit. "Butthey know me. See!"

A light shone from the window of a hut, and swiftly they advanced towards it. Passing through the wall of mud and stone, they found a cheerful company assembled round a glowing fire. An old, old man and woman, with their children and their children's children, and another generation beyond that, all decked out gaily in their holiday attire. The old man, in a voice

that seldom rose above the howling of the wind upon the barren waste, was singing them a Christmas song—it had been a very old song when he was a boy—and from time to time they all joined in the chorus. So surely as they raised their voices, the old man got quite blithe and loud; and so surely as they stopped, his vigour sank again.

The Spirit did not tarry here, but bade Scrooge hold his robe, and passing on above the moor, sped—whither? Not to sea? To sea. To Scrooge's horror, looking back, he saw the last of the land, a frightful range of rocks, behind them; and his ears were deafened by the thundering of water, as it rolled and roared, and raged among the dreadful caverns it had worn, and fiercely tried to undermine the earth.

Built upon a dismal reef of sunken rocks, some league or so from shore, on which the waters chafed and dashed, the wild year through, there stood a solitary lighthouse. Great heaps of sea-weed clung to its base, and storm-birds—born of the wind one might suppose, as sea-weed of the water—rose and fell about it, like the waves they skimmed.

But even here, two men who watched the light had made a fire, that through the loophole in the thick stone wall shed out a ray of brightness on the awful sea. Joining their horny hands over the rough table at which they sat, they wished each other Merry Christmas in their can of grog; and one of them: the elder, too,

with his face all damaged and scarred with hard weather, as the figure-head of an old ship might be: struck up a sturdy song that was like a Gale in itself.

Again the Ghost sped on, above the black and heaving sea—on, on—until, being far away, as he told Scrooge, from any shore, they lighted on a ship. They stood beside the helmsman at the wheel, the look-out in the bow, the officers who had the watch; dark, ghostly figures in their several stations; but every man among them hummed a Christmas tune, or had a Christmas thought, or spoke below his breath to his companion of some bygone Christmas Day, with homeward hopes belonging to it. And every man on board, waking or sleeping, good or bad, had had a kinder word for another on that day than on any day in the year; and had shared to some extent in its festivities; and had remembered those he cared for at a distance, and had known that they delighted to remember him.

It was a great surprise to Scrooge, while listening to the moaning of the wind, and thinking what a solemn thing it was to move on through the lonely darkness over an unknown abyss, whose depths were secrets as profound as Death: it was a great surprise to Scrooge, while thus engaged, to hear a hearty laugh. It was a much greater surprise to Scrooge to recognise it as his own nephew's and to find himself in a bright, dry, gleaming room, with the Spirit standing smiling by his side, and looking at that

same nephew with approving affability!

"Ha, ha!" laughed Scrooge's nephew. "Ha, ha, ha!"

If you should happen, by any unlikely chance, to know a man more blest in a laugh than Scrooge's nephew, all I can say is, I should like to know him too. Introduce him to me, and I'll cultivate his acquaintance.

It is a fair, even-handed, noble adjustment of things, that while there is infection in diseaseand sorrow, there is nothing in the world so irresistibly contagious as laughter and good-humour. When Scrooge's nephew laughed in this way: holding his sides, rolling his head, and twisting his face into the most extravagant contortions: Scrooge's niece, by marriage, laughed as heartily as he. And their assembled friends being not a bit behindhand, roared out lustily.

"Ha, ha! Ha, ha, ha, ha!"

"He said that Christmas was a humbug, as I live!" cried Scrooge's nephew. "He believed it too!"

"More shame for him, Fred!" said Scrooge's niece, indignantly. Bless those women; they never do anything by halves. They are always in earnest.

She was very pretty: exceedingly pretty. With a dimpled, surprised-looking, capital face; a ripe little mouth, that seemed made to be kissed—as no doubt it was; all kinds of good little dots about her chin, that melted into one another when she laughed;

and the sunniest pair of eyes you ever saw in any little creature's head. Altogether she was what you would have called provoking, you know; but satisfactory, too. Oh, perfectly satisfactory.

"He's a comical old fellow," said Scrooge's nephew, "that's the truth: and not so pleasant as he might be. However, his offences carry their own punishment, and I have nothing to say against him."

"I'm sure he is very rich, Fred," hinted Scrooge's niece. "At least you always tell me so."

"What of that, my dear!" said Scrooge's nephew. "His wealth is of no use to him. He don't do any good with it. He don't make himself comfortable with it. He hasn't the satisfaction of thinking—ha, ha, ha!—that he is ever going to benefit US with it."

"I have no patience with him," observed Scrooge's niece. Scrooge's niece's sisters, and all the other ladies, expressed the same opinion.

"Oh, I have!" said Scrooge's nephew. "I am sorry for him; I couldn't be angry with him if I tried. Who suffers by his ill whims! Himself, always. Here, he takes it into his head to dislike us, and he won't come and dine with us. What's the consequence? He don't lose much of a dinner."

"Indeed, I think he loses a very good dinner," interrupted Scrooge's niece. Everybody else said the same, and they must be

allowed to have been competent judges, because they had just had dinner; and, with the dessert upon the table, were clustered round the fire, by lamplight.

"Well! I'm very glad to hear it," said Scrooge's nephew, "because I haven't great faith in these young housekeepers. What do you say, Topper?"

Topper had clearly got his eye upon one of Scrooge's niece's sisters, for he answered that a bachelor was a wretched outcast, who had no right to express an opinion on the subject. Whereat Scrooge's niece's sister—the plump one with the lace tucker: not the one with theroses—blushed.

"Do go on, Fred," said Scrooge's niece, clapping her hands. "He never finishes what he begins to say! He is such a ridiculous fellow!"

Scrooge's nephew revelled in another laugh, and as it was impossible to keep the infection off; though the plump sister tried hard to do it with aromatic vinegar; his example was unanimously followed.

"I was only going to say," said Scrooge's nephew, "that the consequence of his taking a dislike to us, and not making merry with us, is, as I think, that he loses some pleasant moments, which could do him no harm. I am sure he loses pleasanter companions than he can find in his own thoughts, either in his mouldy old office, or his dusty chambers. I mean to give him the same chance

every year, whether he likes it or not, for I pity him. He may rail at Christmas till he dies, but he can't help thinking better of it—I defy him—if he finds me going there, in good temper, year after year, and saying Uncle Scrooge, how are you? If it only puts him in the vein to leave his poor clerk fifty pounds, *that's* something; and I think I shook him yesterday."

It was their turn to laugh now at the notion of his shaking Scrooge. But being thoroughly good-natured, and not much caring what they laughed at, so that they laughed at any rate, he encouraged them in their merriment, and passed the bottle joyously.

After tea, they had some music. For they were a musical family, and knew what they were about, when they sung a Glee or Catch, I can assure you: especially Topper, who could growl away in the bass like a good one, and never swell the large veins in his forehead, or get red in the face over it. Scrooge's niece played well upon the harp; and played among other tunes a simple little air (a mere nothing: you might learn to whistle it in two minutes), which had been familiar to the child who fetched Scrooge from the boarding-school, as he had been reminded by the Ghost of Christmas Past. When this strain of music sounded, all the things that Ghost had shown him, came upon his mind; he softened more and more; and thought that if he could have listened to it often, years ago, he might have cultivated the kindnesses of life

for his own happiness with his own hands, without resorting to the sexton's spade that buried Jacob Marley.

But they didn't devote the whole evening to music. After a while they played at forfeits; for it is good to be children sometimes, and never better than at Christmas, when its mighty Founder was a child himself. Stop! There was first a game at blind-man's buff. Of course there was. And I no more believe Topper was really blind than I believe he had eyes in his boots. My opinion is, that it was a done thing between him and Scrooge's nephew; and that the Ghost of Christmas Present knew it. The way he went after that plump sister in the lace tucker, was an outrage on the credulity of human nature. Knocking down the fire-irons, tumbling over the chairs, bumping against the piano, smothering himself among the curtains, wherever she went, there went he! He always knew where the plump sister was. He wouldn't catch anybody else. If you had fallen up against him (as some of them did), on purpose, he would have made a feint of endeavouring to seize you, which would have been an affront to your understanding, and would instantly have sidled off in the direction of the plump sister.

She often cried out that it wasn't fair; and it really was not. But when at last, he caught her; when, in spite of all her silken rustlings, and her rapid flutterings past him, he got her into a corner whence there was no escape; then his conduct was

the most execrable. For his pretending not to know her; his pretending that it was necessary to touch her head-dress, and further to assure himself of her identity by pressing a certain ring upon her finger, and a certain chain about her neck; was vile, monstrous! No doubt she told him her opinion of it, when, another blind-man being in office, they were so very confidential together, behind the curtains.

Scrooge's niece was not one of the blind-man's buff party, but was made comfortable with a large chair and a footstool, in a snug corner, where the Ghost and Scrooge were close behind her. But she joined in the forfeits, and loved her love to admiration with all the letters of the alphabet. Likewise at the game of How, When, and Where, she was very great, and to the secret joy of Scrooge's nephew, beat her sisters hollow: though they were sharp girls too, as Topper could have told you. There might have been twenty people there, young and old, but they all played, and so did Scrooge; for wholly forgetting in the interest he had in what was going on, that his voice made no sound in their ears, he sometimes came out with his guess quite loud, and very often guessed quite right, too; for the sharpest needle, best Whitechapel, warranted not to cut in the eye, was not sharper than Scrooge; blunt as he took it in his head to be.

The Ghost was greatly pleased to find him in this mood, and looked upon him with such favour, that he begged like a boy to be

allowed to stay until the guests departed. But this the Spirit said could not be done.

"Here is a new game," said Scrooge. "One half hour, Spirit, only one!"

It was a Game called Yes and No, where Scrooge's nephew had to think of something, and the rest must find out what; he only answering to their questions yes or no, as the case was. The brisk fire of questioning to which he was exposed, elicited from him that he was thinking of an animal, a live animal, rather a disagreeable animal, a savage animal, an animal that growled and grunted sometimes, and talked sometimes, and lived in London, and walked about the streets, and wasn't made a show of, and wasn't led by anybody, and didn't live in a menagerie, and was never killed in a market, and was not a horse, or an ass, or a cow, or a bull, or a tiger, or a dog, or a pig, or a cat, or a bear. At every fresh question that was put to him, this nephew burst into a fresh roar of laughter; and was so inexpressibly tickled, that he was obliged to get up off the sofa and stamp. At last the plump sister, falling into a similar state, cried out:

"I have found it out! I know what it is, Fred! I know what it is!"

"What is it?" cried Fred.

"It's your Uncle Scro-o-o-o-oge!"

Which it certainly was. Admiration was the universal sentiment, though some objected that the reply to "Is it a bear?"

ought to have been "Yes;" inasmuch as an answer in the negative was sufficient to have diverted their thoughts from Mr. Scrooge, supposing they had ever had any tendency that way.

"He has given us plenty of merriment, I am sure," said Fred, "and it would be ungrateful not to drink his health. Here is a glass of mulled wine ready to our hand at the moment; and I say, 'Uncle Scrooge!' "

"Well! Uncle Scrooge!" they cried.

"A Merry Christmas and a Happy New Year to the old man, whatever he is!" said Scrooge's nephew. "He wouldn't take it from me, but may he have it, nevertheless. Uncle Scrooge!"

Uncle Scrooge had imperceptibly become so gay and light of heart, that he would have pledged the unconscious company in return, and thanked them in an inaudible speech, if the Ghost had given him time. But the whole scene passed off in the breath of the last word spoken by his nephew; and he and the Spirit were again upon their travels.

Much they saw, and far they went, and many homes they visited, but always with a happy end. The Spirit stood beside sick beds, and they were cheerful; on foreign lands, and they were close at home; by struggling men, and they were patient in their greater hope; by poverty, and it was rich. In almshouse, hospital, and jail, in misery's every refuge, where vain man in his little brief authority had not made fast the door, and barred the Spirit out,

he left his blessing, and taught Scrooge his precepts.

It was a long night, if it were only a night; but Scrooge had his doubts of this, because the Christmas Holidays appeared to be condensed into the space of time they passed together. It was strange, too, that while Scrooge remained unaltered in his outward form, the Ghost grew older, clearly older. Scrooge had observed this change, but never spoke of it, until they left a children's Twelfth Night party, when, looking at the Spirit as they stood together in an open place, he noticed that its hair was grey.

"Are spirits' lives so short?" asked Scrooge.

"My life upon this globe, is very brief," replied the Ghost. "It ends to-night."

"To-night!" cried Scrooge.

"To-night at midnight. Hark! The time is drawing near."

The chimes were ringing the three quarters past eleven at that moment.

"Forgive me if I am not justified in what I ask," said Scrooge, looking intently at the Spirit's robe, "but I see something strange, and not belonging to yourself, protruding from your skirts. Is it a foot or a claw?"

"It might be a claw, for the flesh there is upon it," was the Spirit's sorrowful reply. "Look here."

From the foldings of its robe, it brought two children; wretched, abject, frightful, hideous, miserable. They knelt down

A Christmas Carol

at its feet, and clung upon the outside of its garment.

"Oh, Man! look here. Look, look, down here!" exclaimed the Ghost.

They were a boy and girl. Yellow, meagre, ragged, scowling, wolfish; but prostrate, too, in their humility. Where graceful youth should have filled their features out, and touched them with its freshest tints, a stale and shrivelled hand, like that of age, had pinched, and twisted them, and pulled them into shreds. Where angels might have sat enthroned, devils lurked, and glared out menacing. No change, no degradation, no perversion of humanity, in any grade, through all the mysteries of wonderful creation, has monsters half so horrible and dread.

Scrooge started back, appalled. Having them shown to him in this way, he tried to say they were fine children, but the words choked themselves, rather than be parties to a lie of such enormous magnitude.

"Spirit! are they yours?" Scrooge could say no more.

"They are Man's," said the Spirit, looking down upon them. "And they cling to me, appealing from their fathers. This boy is Ignorance. This girl is Want. Beware them both, and all of their degree, but most of all beware this boy, for on his brow I see that written which is Doom, unless the writing be erased. Deny it!" cried the Spirit, stretching out its hand towards the city. "Slander those who tell it ye! Admit it for your factious purposes, and make

it worse. And bide the end!"

"Have they no refuge or resource?" cried Scrooge.

"Are there no prisons?" said the Spirit, turning on him for the last time with his own words. "Are there no workhouses?"

The bell struck twelve.

Scrooge looked about him for the Ghost, and saw it not. As the last stroke ceased to vibrate, he remembered the prediction of old Jacob Marley, and lifting up his eyes, beheld a solemn Phantom, draped and hooded, coming, like a mist along the ground, towards him.

STAVE IV

THE LAST OF THE SPIRITS

The Phantom slowly, gravely, silently, approached. When it came near him, Scrooge bent down upon his knee; for in the very air through which this Spirit moved it seemed to scatter gloom and mystery.

It was shrouded in a deep black garment, which concealed its head, its face, its form, and left nothing of it visible save one outstretched hand. But for this it would have been difficult to detach its figure from the night, and separate it from the darkness by which it was surrounded.

He felt that it was tall and stately when it came beside him, and that its mysterious presence filled him with a solemn dread. He knew no more, for the Spirit neither spoke nor moved.

"I am in the presence of the Ghost of Christmas Yet To Come?" said Scrooge.

The Spirit answered not, but pointed onward with its hand.

"You are about to show me shadows of the things that have not happened, but will happen in the time before us," Scrooge

pursued. "Is that so, Spirit?"

The upper portion of the garment was contracted for an instant in its folds, as if the Spirit had inclined its head. That was the only answer he received.

Although well used to ghostly company by this time, Scrooge feared the silent shape so much that his legs trembled beneath him, and he found that he could hardly stand when he prepared to follow it. The Spirit paused a moment, as observing his condition, and givinghim time to recover.

But Scrooge was all the worse for this. It thrilled him with a vague uncertain horror, to know that behind the dusky shroud, there were ghostly eyes intently fixed upon him, while he, though he stretched his own to the utmost, could see nothing but a spectral hand and one great heap of black.

"Ghost of the Future!" he exclaimed, "I fear you more than any spectre I have seen. But as I know your purpose is to do me good, and as I hope to live to be another man from what Iwas, I am prepared to bear you company, and do it with a thankful heart. Will you not speak to me?"

It gave him no reply. The hand was pointed straight before them.

"Lead on!" said Scrooge. "Lead on! The night is waning fast, and it is precious time to me, I know. Lead on, Spirit!"

The Phantom moved away as it had come towards him.

Scrooge followed in the shadow of its dress, which bore him up, he thought, and carried him along.

They scarcely seemed to enter the city; for the city rather seemed to spring up about them, and encompass them of its own act. But there they were, in the heart of it; on 'Change, amongst the merchants; who hurried up and down, and chinked the money in their pockets, and conversed in groups, and looked at their watches, and trifled thoughtfully with their great gold seals; and so forth, as Scrooge had seen them often.

The Spirit stopped beside one little knot of business men. Observing that the hand was pointed to them, Scrooge advanced to listen to their talk.

"No," said a great fat man with a monstrous chin, "I don't know much about it, either way. I only know he's dead."

"When did he die?" inquired another.

"Last night, I believe."

"Why, what was the matter with him?" asked a third, taking a vast quantity of snuff out of a very large snuff-box. "I thought he'd never die."

"God knows," said the first, with a yawn.

"What has he done with his money?" asked a red-faced gentleman with a pendulous excrescence on the end of his nose, that shook like the gills of a turkey-cock.

"I haven't heard," said the man with the large chin, yawning

again. "Left it to his company, perhaps. He hasn't left it to *me*. That's all I know."

This pleasantry was received with a general laugh.

"It's likely to be a very cheap funeral," said the same speaker; "for upon my life I don't know of anybody to go to it. Suppose we make up a party and volunteer?"

"I don't mind going if a lunch is provided," observed the gentleman with the excrescence on his nose. "But I must be fed, if I make one."

Another laugh.

"Well, I am the most disinterested among you, after all," said the first speaker, "for I never wear black gloves, and I never eat lunch. But I'll offer to go, if anybody else will. When I come to think of it, I'm not at all sure that I wasn't his most particular friend; for we used to stop and speak whenever we met. Bye, bye!"

Speakers and listeners strolled away, and mixed with other groups. Scrooge knew the men, and looked towards the Spirit for an explanation.

The Phantom glided on into a street. Its finger pointed to two persons meeting. Scrooge listened again, thinking that the explanation might lie here.

He knew these men, also, perfectly. They were men of business: very wealthy, and of great importance. He had made a

point always of standing well in their esteem: in a business point of view, that is; strictly in a business point of view.

"How are you?" said one.

"How are you?" returned the other.

"Well!" said the first. "Old Scratch has got his own at last, hey?"

"So I am told," returned the second. "Cold, isn't it?"

"Seasonable for Christmas time. You're not a skater, I suppose?"

"No. No. Something else to think of. Good morning!"

Not another word. That was their meeting, their conversation, and their parting.

Scrooge was at first inclined to be surprised that the Spirit should attach importance to conversations apparently so trivial; but feeling assured that they must have some hidden purpose, he set himself to consider what it was likely to be. They could scarcely be supposed to have any bearing on the death of Jacob, his old partner, for that was Past, and this Ghost's province was the Future. Nor could he think of any one immediately connected with himself, to whom he could apply them. But nothing doubting that to whomsoever they applied they had some latent moral for his own improvement, he resolved to treasure up every word he heard, and everything he saw; and especially to observe the shadow of himself when it appeared. For he had an

expectation that the conduct of his future self would give him the clue he missed, and would render the solution of these riddles easy.

He looked about in that very place for his own image; but another man stood in his accustomed corner, and though the clock pointed to his usual time of day for being there, he saw no likeness of himself among the multitudes that poured in through the Porch. It gave him little surprise, however; for he had been revolving in his mind a change of life, and thought and hoped he saw his new-born resolutions carried out in this.

Quiet and dark, beside him stood the Phantom, with its outstretched hand. When he roused himself from his thoughtful quest, he fancied from the turn of the hand, and its situation in reference to himself, that the Unseen Eyes were looking at him keenly. It made him shudder, and feel very cold.

They left the busy scene, and went into an obscure part of the town, where Scrooge had never penetrated before, although he recognised its situation, and its bad repute. The ways were foul and narrow; the shops and houses wretched; the people half-naked, drunken, slipshod, ugly. Alleys and archways, like so many cesspools, disgorged their offences of smell, and dirt, and life, upon the straggling streets; and the whole quarter reeked with crime, with filth, and misery.

Far in this den of infamous resort, there was a low-browed,

beetling shop, below a pent-house roof, where iron, old rags, bottles, bones, and greasy offal, were bought. Upon the floor within, were piled up heaps of rusty keys, nails, chains, hinges, files, scales, weights, and refuse iron of all kinds. Secrets that few would like to scrutinise were bred and hidden in mountains of unseemly rags, masses of corrupted fat, and sepulchres of bones. Sitting in among the wares he dealt in, by a charcoal stove, made of old bricks, was a grey-haired rascal, nearly seventy years of age; who had screened himself from the cold air without, by a frousy curtaining of miscellaneous tatters, hung upon a line; and smoked his pipe in all the luxury of calm retirement.

Scrooge and the Phantom came into the presence of this man, just as a woman with a heavy bundle slunk into the shop. But she had scarcely entered, when another woman, similarly laden, came in too; and she was closely followed by a man in faded black, who was no less startled by the sight of them, than they had been upon the recognition of each other. After ashort period of blank astonishment, in which the old man with the pipe had joined them, they all three burst into a laugh.

"Let the charwoman alone to be the first!" cried she who had entered first. "Let the laundress alone to be the second; and let the undertaker's man alone to be the third. Look here, old Joe, here's a chance! If we haven't all three met here without meaning it!"

"You couldn't have met in a better place," said old Joe, removing his pipe from his mouth.

"Come into the parlour. You were made free of it long ago, you know; and the other two an't strangers. Stop till I shut the door of the shop. Ah! How it skreeks! There an't such a rusty bit of metal in the place as its own hinges, I believe; and I'm sure there's no such old bones here, as mine. Ha, ha! We're all suitable to our calling, we're well matched. Come into the parlour. Come into the parlour."

The parlour was the space behind the screen of rags. The old man raked the fire together with an old stair-rod, and having trimmed his smoky lamp (for it was night), with the stem of his pipe, put it in his mouth again.

While he did this, the woman who had already spoken threw her bundle on the floor, and sat down in a flaunting manner on a stool; crossing her elbows on her knees, and looking with a bold defiance at the other two.

"What odds then! What odds, Mrs. Dilber?" said the woman. "Every person has a right to take care of themselves. *He* always did."

"That's true, indeed!" said the laundress. "No man more so."

"Why then, don't stand staring as if you was afraid, woman; who's the wiser? We're not going to pick holes in each other's coats, I suppose?"

"No, indeed!" said Mrs. Dilber and the man together. "We should hope not."

"Very well, then!" cried the woman. "That's enough. Who's the worse for the loss of a few things like these? Not a dead man, I suppose."

"No, indeed," said Mrs. Dilber, laughing.

"If he wanted to keep 'em after he was dead, a wicked old screw," pursued the woman, "why wasn't he natural in his lifetime? If he had been, he'd have had somebody to look after him when he was struck with Death, instead of lying gasping out his last there, alone by himself."

"It's the truest word that ever was spoke," said Mrs. Dilber. "It's a judgment on him."

"I wish it was a little heavier judgment," replied the woman; "and it should have been, you may depend upon it, if I could have laid my hands on anything else. Open that bundle, old Joe, and let me know the value of it. Speak out plain. I'm not afraid to be the first, nor afraid for them to see it. We know pretty well that we were helping ourselves, before we met here, I believe. It's no sin. Open the bundle, Joe."

But the gallantry of her friends would not allow of this; and the man in faded black, mounting the breach first, produced his plunder. It was not extensive. A seal or two, a pencil-case, a pair of sleeve-buttons, and a brooch of no great value, were all. They

were severally examined and appraised by old Joe, who chalked the sums he was disposed to give for each, upon the wall, and added them up into a total when he found there was nothing more to come.

"That's your account," said Joe, "and I wouldn't give another sixpence, if I was to be boiled for not doing it. Who's next?"

Mrs. Dilber was next. Sheets and towels, a little wearing apparel, two old-fashioned silver teaspoons, a pair of sugar-tongs, and a few boots. Her account was stated on the wall in the same manner.

"I always give too much to ladies. It's a weakness of mine, and that's the way I ruin myself," said old Joe. "That's your account. If you asked me for another penny, and made it an open question, I'd repent of being so liberal and knock off half-a-crown."

"And now undo my bundle, Joe," said the first woman.

Joe went down on his knees for the greater convenience of opening it, and having unfastened a great many knots, dragged out a large and heavy roll of some dark stuff.

"What do you call this?" said Joe. "Bed-curtains!"

"Ah!" returned the woman, laughing and leaning forward on her crossed arms. "Bed-curtains!"

"You don't mean to say you took 'em down, rings and all, with him lying there?" said Joe.

"Yes I do," replied the woman. "Why not?"

"You were born to make your fortune," said Joe, "and you'll certainly do it."

"I certainly shan't hold my hand, when I can get anything in it by reaching it out, for the sake of such a man as He was, I promise you, Joe," returned the woman coolly. "Don't drop that oil upon the blankets, now."

"His blankets?" asked Joe.

"Whose else's do you think?" replied the woman. "He isn't likely to take cold without 'em, I dare say."

"I hope he didn't die of anything catching? Eh?" said old Joe, stopping in his work, and looking up.

"Don't you be afraid of that," returned the woman. "I an't so fond of his company that I'd loiter about him for such things, if he did. Ah! you may look through that shirt till your eyes ache; but you won't find a hole in it, nor a threadbare place. It's the best he had, and a fine one too. They'd have wasted it, if it hadn't been for me."

"What do you call wasting of it?" asked old Joe.

"Putting it on him to be buried in, to be sure," replied the woman with a laugh. "Somebody was fool enough to do it, but I took it off again. If calico an't good enough for such a purpose, it isn't good enough for anything. It's quite as becoming to the body. He can't look uglier than he did in that one."

Scrooge listened to this dialogue in horror. As they sat grouped

about their spoil, in the scanty light afforded by the old man's lamp, he viewed them with a detestation and disgust, which could hardly have been greater, though they had been obscene demons, marketing the corpse itself.

"Ha, ha!" laughed the same woman, when old Joe, producing a flannel bag with money in it, told out their several gains upon the ground. "This is the end of it, you see! He frightened every one away from him when he was alive, to profit us when he was dead! Ha, ha, ha!"

"Spirit!" said Scrooge, shuddering from head to foot. "I see, I see. The case of this unhappy man might be my own. My life tends that way, now. Merciful Heaven, what is this!"

He recoiled in terror, for the scene had changed, and now he almost touched a bed: a bare, uncurtained bed: on which, beneath a ragged sheet, there lay a something covered up, which, though it was dumb, announced itself in awful language.

The room was very dark, too dark to be observed with any accuracy, though Scrooge glanced round it in obedience to a secret impulse, anxious to know what kind of room it was. A pale light, rising in the outer air, fell straight upon the bed; and on it, plundered and bereft, unwatched, unwept, uncared for, was the body of this man.

Scrooge glanced towards the Phantom. Its steady hand was pointed to the head. The cover was so carelessly adjusted that the

slightest raising of it, the motion of a finger upon Scrooge's part, would have disclosed the face. He thought of it, felt how easy it would be to do, and longed to do it; but had no more power to withdraw the veil than to dismiss the spectre at his side.

Oh cold, cold, rigid, dreadful Death, set up thine altar here, and dress it with such terrors as thou hast at thy command: for this is thy dominion! But of the loved, revered, and honoured head, thou canst not turn one hair to thy dread purposes, or make one feature odious. It is not that the hand is heavy and will fall down when released; it is not that the heart and pulse are still; but that the hand was open, generous, and true; the heart brave, warm, and tender; and the pulse a man's. Strike, Shadow, strike! And see his good deeds springing from the wound, to sow the world with life immortal!

No voice pronounced these words in Scrooge's ears, and yet he heard them when he looked upon the bed. He thought, if this man could be raised up now, what would be his foremost thoughts? Avarice, hard-dealing, griping cares? They have brought him to a rich end, truly! He lay, in the dark empty house, with not a man, a woman, or a child, to say that he was kind to me in this or that, and for the memory of one kind word I will be kind to him. A cat was tearing at the door, and there was a sound of gnawing rats beneath the hearth-stone. What they wanted in the room of death, and why they were so restless and disturbed,

Scrooge did not dare to think.

"Spirit!" he said, "this is a fearful place. In leaving it, I shall not leave its lesson, trust me. Let us go!"

Still the Ghost pointed with an unmoved finger to the head.

"I understand you," Scrooge returned, "and I would do it, if I could. But I have not the power, Spirit. I have not the power."

Again it seemed to look upon him.

"If there is any person in the town, who feels emotion caused by this man's death," said Scrooge quite agonised, "show that person to me, Spirit, I beseech you!"

The Phantom spread its dark robe before him for a moment, like a wing; and withdrawing it, revealed a room by daylight, where a mother and her children were.

She was expecting some one, and with anxious eagerness; for she walked up and down the room; started at every sound; looked out from the window; glanced at the clock; tried, but invain, to work with her needle; and could hardly bear the voices of the children in their play. At length the long-expected knock was heard. She hurried to the door, and met her husband; a man whose face was careworn and depressed, though he was young. There was a remarkable expression in it now; a kind of serious delight of which he felt ashamed, and which he struggled to repress.

He sat down to the dinner that had been hoarding for him by

the fire; and when she asked him faintly what news (which was not until after a long silence), he appeared embarrassed how to answer.

"Is it good?" she said, "or bad?"—to help him.

"Bad," he answered.

"We are quite ruined?"

"No. There is hope yet, Caroline."

"If he relents," she said, amazed, "there is! Nothing is past hope, if such a miracle has happened."

"He is past relenting," said her husband. "He is dead."

She was a mild and patient creature if her face spoke truth; but she was thankful in her soul to hear it, and she said so, with clasped hands. She prayed forgiveness the next moment, and was sorry; but the first was the emotion of her heart.

"What the half-drunken woman whom I told you of last night, said to me, when I tried to see him and obtain a week's delay; and what I thought was a mere excuse to avoid me; turns out to have been quite true. He was not only very ill, but dying, then."

"To whom will our debt be transferred?"

"I don't know. But before that time we shall be ready with the money; and even though we were not, it would be a bad fortune indeed to find so merciless a creditor in his successor. We may sleep to-night with light hearts, Caroline!"

Yes. Soften it as they would, their hearts were lighter. The

children's faces, hushed and clustered round to hear what they so little understood, were brighter; and it was a happier house for this man's death! The only emotion that the Ghost could show him, caused by the event, was one of pleasure.

"Let me see some tenderness connected with a death," said Scrooge; "or that dark chamber, Spirit, which we left just now, will be for ever present to me."

The Ghost conducted him through several streets familiar to his feet; and as they went along, Scrooge looked here and there to find himself, but nowhere was he to be seen. They entered poor Bob Cratchit's house; the dwelling he had visited before; and found the mother and the children seated round the fire.

Quiet. Very quiet. The noisy little Cratchits were as still as statues in one corner, and sat looking up at Peter, who had a book before him. The mother and her daughters were engaged in sewing. But surely they were very quiet!

" 'And He took a child, and set him in the midst of them.' "

Where had Scrooge heard those words? He had not dreamed them. The boy must have read them out, as he and the Spirit crossed the threshold. Why did he not go on?

The mother laid her work upon the table, and put her hand up to her face.

"The colour hurts my eyes," she said.

The colour? Ah, poor Tiny Tim!

"They're better now again," said Cratchit's wife. "It makes them weak by candle-light; and I wouldn't show weak eyes to your father when he comes home, for the world. It must be near his time."

"Past it rather," Peter answered, shutting up his book. "But I think he has walked a little slower than he used, these few last evenings, mother."

They were very quiet again. At last she said, and in a steady, cheerful voice, that only faltered once:

"I have known him walk with—I have known him walk with Tiny Tim upon his shoulder, very fast indeed."

"And so have I," cried Peter. "Often."

"And so have I," exclaimed another. So had all.

"But he was very light to carry," she resumed, intent upon her work, "and his father loved him so, that it was no trouble: no trouble. And there is your father at the door!"

She hurried out to meet him; and little Bob in his comforter— he had need of it, poor fellow—came in. His tea was ready for him on the hob, and they all tried who should help him to it most. Then the two young Cratchits got upon his knees and laid, each child a little cheek, against his face, as if they said, "Don't mind it, father. Don't be grieved!"

Bob was very cheerful with them, and spoke pleasantly to all the family. He looked at the work upon the table, and praised the

industry and speed of Mrs. Cratchit and the girls. They would be done long before Sunday, he said.

"Sunday! You went to-day, then, Robert?" said his wife.

"Yes, my dear," returned Bob. "I wish you could have gone. It would have done you good to see how green a place it is. But you'll see it often. I promised him that I would walk there on a Sunday. My little, little child!" cried Bob. "My little child!"

He broke down all at once. He couldn't help it. If he could have helped it, he and his child would have been farther apart perhaps than they were.

He left the room, and went up-stairs into the room above, which was lighted cheerfully, and hung with Christmas. There was a chair set close beside the child, and there were signs of some one having been there, lately. Poor Bob sat down in it, and when he had thought a little and composed himself, he kissed the little face. He was reconciled to what had happened, and went down again quite happy.

They drew about the fire, and talked; the girls and mother working still. Bob told them of the extraordinary kindness of Mr. Scrooge's nephew, whom he had scarcely seen but once, and who, meeting him in the street that day, and seeing that he looked a little—"just a little down you know," said Bob, inquired what had happened to distress him. "On which," said Bob, "for he is the pleasantest-spoken gentleman you ever heard, I told him. 'I

am heartily sorry for it, Mr. Cratchit,' he said, 'and heartily sorry for your good wife.' By the bye, how he ever knew that , I don't know."

"Knew what, my dear?"

"Why, that you were a good wife," replied Bob.

"Everybody knows that!" said Peter.

"Very well observed, my boy!" cried Bob. "I hope they do. 'Heartily sorry,' he said, 'for your good wife. If I can be of service to you in any way,' he said, giving me his card, 'that's where I live. Pray come to me.' Now, it wasn't," cried Bob, "for the sake of anything he might be able to do for us, so much as for his kind way, that this was quite delightful. It really seemed as if he had known our Tiny Tim, and felt with us."

"I'm sure he's a good soul!" said Mrs. Cratchit.

"You would be surer of it, my dear," returned Bob, "if you saw and spoke to him. I shouldn't be at all surprised—mark what I say!—if he got Peter a better situation."

"Only hear that, Peter," said Mrs. Cratchit.

"And then," cried one of the girls, "Peter will be keeping company with some one, and setting up for himself."

"Get along with you!" retorted Peter, grinning.

"It's just as likely as not," said Bob, "one of these days; though there's plenty of time for that, my dear. But however and whenever we part from one another, I am sure we shall none of us

forget poor Tiny Tim—shall we—or this first parting that there was among us?"

"Never, father!" cried they all.

"And I know," said Bob, "I know, my dears, that when we recollect how patient and how mild he was; although he was a little, little child; we shall not quarrel easily among ourselves, and forget poor Tiny Tim in doing it."

"No, never, father!" they all cried again.

"I am very happy," said little Bob, "I am very happy!"

Mrs. Cratchit kissed him, his daughters kissed him, the two young Cratchits kissed him, and Peter and himself shook hands. Spirit of Tiny Tim, thy childish essence was from God!

"Spectre," said Scrooge, "something informs me that our parting moment is at hand. I know it, but I know not how. Tell me what man that was whom we saw lying dead?"

The Ghost of Christmas Yet To Come conveyed him, as before—though at a different time, he thought: indeed, there seemed no order in these latter visions, save that they were in the Future—into the resorts of business men, but showed him not himself. Indeed, the Spirit did not stay for anything, but went straight on, as to the end just now desired, until besought by Scrooge to tarry for a moment.

"This court," said Scrooge, "through which we hurry now, is where my place of occupation is, and has been for a length of

time. I see the house. Let me behold what I shall be, in days to come!"

The Spirit stopped; the hand was pointed elsewhere.

"The house is yonder," Scrooge exclaimed. "Why do you point away?"

The inexorable finger underwent no change.

Scrooge hastened to the window of his office, and looked in. It was an office still, but not his. The furniture was not the same, and the figure in the chair was not himself. The Phantom pointed as before.

He joined it once again, and wondering why and whither he had gone, accompanied it until they reached an iron gate. He paused to look round before entering.

A churchyard. Here, then; the wretched man whose name he had now to learn, lay underneath the ground. It was a worthy place. Walled in by houses; overrun by grass and weeds, the growth of vegetation's death, not life; choked up with too much burying; fat with repleted appetite. A worthy place!

The Spirit stood among the graves, and pointed down to One. He advanced towards it trembling. The Phantom was exactly as it had been, but he dreaded that he saw new meaningin its solemn shape.

"Before I draw nearer to that stone to which you point," said Scrooge, "answer me one question. Are these the shadows of the

things that Will be, or are they shadows of things that May be, only?"

Still the Ghost pointed downward to the grave by which it stood.

"Men's courses will foreshadow certain ends, to which, if persevered in, they must lead," said Scrooge. "But if the courses be departed from, the ends will change. Say it is thus with what you show me!"

The Spirit was immovable as ever.

Scrooge crept towards it, trembling as he went; and following the finger, read upon the stone of the neglected grave his own name, Ebenezer Scrooge.

"Am I that man who lay upon the bed?" he cried, upon his knees.

The finger pointed from the grave to him, and back again.

"No, Spirit! Oh no, no!"

The finger still was there.

"Spirit!" he cried, tight clutching at its robe, "hear me! I am not the man I was. I will not be the man I must have been but for this intercourse. Why show me this, if I am past all hope!"

For the first time the hand appeared to shake.

"Good Spirit," he pursued, as down upon the ground he fell before it: "Your nature intercedes for me, and pities me. Assure me that I yet may change these shadows you have shown me, by

an altered life!"

The kind hand trembled.

"I will honour Christmas in my heart, and try to keep it all the year. I will live in the Past, the Present, and the Future. The Spirits of all Three shall strive within me. I will not shut out the lessons that they teach. Oh, tell me I may sponge away the writing on this stone!"

In his agony, he caught the spectral hand. It sought to free itself, but he was strong in his entreaty, and detained it. The Spirit, stronger yet, repulsed him.

Holding up his hands in a last prayer to have his fate reversed, he saw an alteration in the Phantom's hood and dress. It shrunk, collapsed, and dwindled down into a bedpost.

STAVE V

⁘⟨✦⟩⁘

THE END OF IT

Yes! and the bedpost was his own. The bed was his own, the room was his own. Best and happiest of all, the Time before him was his own, to make amends in!

"I will live in the Past, the Present, and the Future!" Scrooge repeated, as he scrambled out of bed. "The Spirits of all Three shall strive within me. Oh Jacob Marley! Heaven, and the Christmas Time be praised for this! I say it on my knees, old Jacob; on my knees!"

He was so fluttered and so glowing with his good intentions, that his broken voice would scarcely answer to his call. He had been sobbing violently in his conflict with the Spirit, and his face was wet with tears.

"They are not torn down," cried Scrooge, folding one of his bed-curtains in his arms, "they are not torn down, rings and all. They are here—I am here—the shadows of the things that would have been, may be dispelled. They will be. I know they will!"

His hands were busy with his garments all this time; turning them inside out, putting them on upside down, tearing

them, mislaying them, making them parties to every kind of extravagance.

"I don't know what to do!" cried Scrooge, laughing and crying in the same breath; and making a perfect Laocoön of himself with his stockings. "I am as light as a feather, I am as happy as an angel, I am as merry as a school-boy. I am as giddy as a drunken man. A merry Christmas to everybody! A happy New Year to all the world. Hallo here! Whoop! Hallo!"

He had frisked into the sitting-room, and was now standing there: perfectly winded.

"There's the saucepan that the gruel was in!" cried Scrooge, starting off again, and going round the fireplace. "There's the door, by which the Ghost of Jacob Marley entered! There's the corner where the Ghost of Christmas Present, sat! There's the window where I saw the wandering Spirits! It's all right, it's all true, it all happened. Ha ha ha!"

Really, for a man who had been out of practice for so many years, it was a splendid laugh, a most illustrious laugh. The father of a long, long line of brilliant laughs!

"I don't know what day of the month it is!" said Scrooge. "I don't know how long I've been among the Spirits. I don't know anything. I'm quite a baby. Never mind. I don't care. I'd rather be a baby. Hallo! Whoop! Hallo here!"

He was checked in his transports by the churches ringing out

the lustiest peals he had ever heard. Clash, clang, hammer; ding, dong, bell. Bell, dong, ding; hammer, clang, clash! Oh, glorious, glorious!

Running to the window, he opened it, and put out his head. No fog, no mist; clear, bright, jovial, stirring, cold; cold, piping for the blood to dance to; Golden sunlight; Heavenly sky; sweet fresh air; merry bells. Oh, glorious! Glorious!

"What's to-day!" cried Scrooge, calling downward to a boy in Sunday clothes, who perhaps had loitered in to look about him.

"Eh?" returned the boy, with all his might of wonder.

"What's to-day, my fine fellow?" said Scrooge.

"To-day!" replied the boy. "Why, Christmas Day."

"It's Christmas Day!" said Scrooge to himself. "I haven't missed it. The Spirits have done it all in one night. They can do anything they like. Of course they can. Of course they can. Hallo, my fine fellow!"

"Hallo!" returned the boy.

"Do you know the Poulterer's, in the next street but one, at the corner?" Scrooge inquired.

"I should hope I did," replied the lad.

An intelligent boy!" said Scrooge. "A remarkable boy! Do you know whether they've sold the prize Turkey that was hanging up there?—Not the little prize Turkey: the big one?"

"What, the one as big as me?" returned the boy.

"What a delightful boy!" said Scrooge. "It's a pleasure to talk to him. Yes, my buck!"

"It's hanging there now," replied the boy.

"Is it?" said Scrooge. "Go and buy it."

"Walk-ER!" exclaimed the boy.

"No, no," said Scrooge, "I am in earnest. Go and buy it, and tell 'em to bring it here, that I may give them the direction where to take it. Come back with the man, and I'll give you a shilling. Come back with him in less than five minutes and I'll give you half-a-crown!"

The boy was off like a shot. He must have had a steady hand at a trigger who could have got a shot off half so fast.

"I'll send it to Bob Cratchit's!" whispered Scrooge, rubbing his hands, and splitting with a laugh. "He sha'n't know who sends it. It's twice the size of Tiny Tim. Joe Miller never made such a joke as sending it to Bob's will be!"

The hand in which he wrote the address was not a steady one, but write it he did, somehow, and went down-stairs to open the street door, ready for the coming of the poulterer's man. As he stood there, waiting his arrival, the knocker caught his eye.

"I shall love it, as long as I live!" cried Scrooge, patting it with his hand. "I scarcely ever looked at it before. What an honest expression it has in its face! It's a wonderful knocker!—Here's the Turkey! Hallo! Whoop! How are you! Merry Christmas!"

It *was* a Turkey! He never could have stood upon his legs, that bird. He would have snapped 'em short off in a minute, like sticks of sealing-wax.

"Why, it's impossible to carry that to Camden Town,"said Scrooge. "You must have a cab."

The chuckle with which he said this, and the chuckle with which he paid for the Turkey, and the chuckle with which he paid for the cab, and the chuckle with which he recompensed the boy, were only to be exceeded by the chuckle with which he sat down breathless in his chair again, and chuckled till he cried.

Shaving was not an easy task, for his hand continued to shake very much; and shaving requires attention, even when you don't dance while you are at it. But if he had cut the end of his nose off, he would have put a piece of sticking-plaister over it, and been quite satisfied.

He dressed himself "all in his best," and at last got out into the streets. The people were by this time pouring forth, as he had seen them with the Ghost of Christmas Present; and walking with his hands behind him, Scrooge regarded every one with a delighted smile. He looked so irresistibly pleasant, in a word, that three or four good-humoured fellows said, "Good morning, sir! A merry Christmas to you!" And Scrooge said often afterwards, that of all the blithe sounds he had ever heard, those were the blithest in his ears.

He had not gone far, when coming on towards him he beheld the portly gentleman, who had walked into his counting-house the day before, and said, "Scrooge and Marley's, I believe?" It sent a pang across his heart to think how this old gentleman would look upon him when they met; but he knew what path lay straight before him, and he took it.

"My dear sir," said Scrooge, quickening his pace, and taking the old gentleman by both his hands. "How do you do? I hope you succeeded yesterday. It was very kind of you. A merry Christmas to you, sir!"

"Mr. Scrooge?"

"Yes," said Scrooge. "That is my name, and I fear it may not be pleasant to you. Allow me to ask your pardon. And will you have the goodness"—here Scrooge whispered in his ear.

"Lord bless me!" cried the gentleman, as if his breath were taken away. "My dear Mr. Scrooge, are you serious?"

"If you please," said Scrooge. "Not a farthing less. A great many back-payments are included in it, I assure you. Will you do me that favour?"

"My dear sir," said the other, shaking hands with him. "I don't know what to say to such munifi—"

"Don't say anything, please," retorted Scrooge. "Come and see me. Will you come and see me?"

"I will!" cried the old gentleman. And it was clear he meant to

do it.

"Thank'ee," said Scrooge. "I am much obliged to you.I thank you fifty times. Bless you!"

He went to church, and walked about the streets, and watched the people hurrying to and fro, and patted children on the head, and questioned beggars, and looked down into the kitchens of houses, and up to the windows, and found that everything could yield him pleasure. He had never dreamed that any walk—that anything—could give him so much happiness. In the afternoon he turned his steps towards his nephew's house.

He passed the door a dozen times, before he had the courage to go up and knock. But he made a dash, and did it:

"Is your master at home, my dear?" said Scrooge to the girl. Nice girl! Very.

"Yes, sir."

"Where is he, my love?" said Scrooge.

"He's in the dining-room, sir, along with mistress. I'll show you up-stairs, if you please."

"Thank'ee. He knows me," said Scrooge, with his hand already on the dining-room lock. "I'll go in here, my dear."

He turned it gently, and sidled his face in, round the door. They were looking at the table (which was spread out in great array); for these young housekeepers are always nervous on such points, and like to see that everything is right.

"Fred!" said Scrooge.

Dear heart alive, how his niece by marriage started! Scrooge had forgotten, for the moment, about her sitting in the corner with the footstool, or he wouldn't have done it, on any account.

"Why bless my soul!" cried Fred, "who's that?"

"It's I. Your uncle Scrooge. I have come to dinner. Will you let me in, Fred?"

Let him in! It is a mercy he didn't shake his arm off. He was at home in five minutes. Nothing could be heartier. His niece looked just the same. So did Topper when he came. So did the plump sister when she came. So did every one when they came. Wonderful party, wonderful games, wonderful unanimity, wonder-ful happiness!

But he was early at the office next morning. Oh, he was early there. If he could only be there first, and catch Bob Cratchit coming late! That was the thing he had set his heart upon.

And he did it; yes, he did! The clock struck nine. No Bob. A quarter past. No Bob. He was full eighteen minutes and a half behind his time. Scrooge sat with his door wide open, that he might see him come into the Tank.

His hat was off, before he opened the door; his comforter too. He was on his stool in a jiffy; driving away with his pen, as if he were trying to overtake nine o'clock.

"Hallo!" growled Scrooge, in his accustomed voice, as near as

he could feign it. "What do you mean by coming here at this time of day?"

I am very sorry, sir," said Bob. "I am behind my time."

"You are?" repeated Scrooge. "Yes. I think you are. Step this way, sir, if you please."

"It's only once a year, sir," pleaded Bob, appearing from the Tank. "It shall not be repeated. I was making rather merry yesterday, sir."

"Now, I'll tell you what, my friend," said Scrooge, "I am not going to stand this sort of thing any longer. And therefore," he continued, leaping from his stool, and giving Bob such a dig in the waistcoat that he staggered back into the Tank again; "and therefore I am about to raise your salary!"

Bob trembled, and got a little nearer to the ruler. He had a momentary idea of knocking Scrooge down with it, holding him, and calling to the people in the court for help and a strait-waistcoat.

"A merry Christmas, Bob!" said Scrooge, with an earnestness that could not be mistaken, as he clapped him on the back. "A merrier Christmas, Bob, my good fellow, than I have given you, for many a year! I'll raise your salary, and endeavour to assist your struggling family, and we will discuss your affairs this very afternoon, over a Christmas bowl of smoking bishop, Bob! Make up the fires, and buy another coal-scuttle before you dot another i,

Bob Cratchit!"

Scrooge was better than his word. He did it all, and infinitely more; and to Tiny Tim, who did not die, he was a second father. He became as good a friend, as good a master, and as good a man, as the good old city knew, or any other good old city, town, or borough, in the good old world. Some people laughed to see the alteration in him, but he let them laugh, and little heeded them; for he was wise enough to know that nothing ever happened on this globe, for good, at which some people did not have their fill of laughter in the outset; and knowing that such as these would be blind anyway, he thought it quite as well that they should wrinkle up their eyes in grins, as have the malady in less attractive forms. His own heart laughed: and that was quite enough for him.

He had no further intercourse with Spirits, but lived upon the Total Abstinence Principle, ever afterwards; and it was always said of him, that he knew how to keep Christmas well, if any man alive possessed the knowledge. May that be truly said of us, and all of us! And so, as Tiny Tim observed, God bless Us, Every One!

圖片說明：

＊〈馬利的鬼魂〉（*Marley's ghost*）

Illustration by John Leech(1817-64)

作者：約翰・李奇

圖片來源：Universal History Archive／UIG／The Bridgeman Art Library

＊〈現在的聖誕精靈〉（*The Ghost of Christmas Present*）

Illustration by John Leech (1817-64)

作者：約翰・李奇

圖片來源：Universal History Archive／UIG／The Bridgeman Art Library

＊〈費茲維先生〉（*Mr. Fezziwig's Ball*, engraving）

作者：約翰・李奇（John Leech）。

圖片來源：Victoria & Albert Museum, London, UK／The Bridgeman Art Library